Baylor didn't war̲ but he sensed someone had been in Mariah's room.

"What woke you?" Baylor asked as he slid the screen closed and sat down on the hearth.

"The back door was wide open and banging against the doorjamb in the wind."

Could the figure she'd seen outside be the person who'd made the tracks in her room? He didn't know for sure, but he wouldn't relax until he got Mariah safely off the mountain.

"Get some rest." He moved away from her, closer to the chair next to the fireplace, to stand guard, and watched her close her beautiful blue eyes.

Whatever was going on at the Bellwether Ranch was his problem; he wasn't about to get her involved.

JAN HAMBRIGHT

The HIGH COUNTRY RANCHER

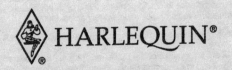

HARLEQUIN®

TORONTO • NEW YORK • LONDON
AMSTERDAM • PARIS • SYDNEY • HAMBURG
STOCKHOLM • ATHENS • TOKYO • MILAN • MADRID
PRAGUE • WARSAW • BUDAPEST • AUCKLAND

To my editor, Allison.
Thank you for making me push myself.

To my family, who endured too many chili nights
while I worked late. You're the best! Love Ya.

And to my friend Ellen, for the great pictures
you took of my horse Texas,
who may or may not have made the book's cover. Smiles.

ISBN-13: 978-0-373-69385-6
ISBN-10:   0-373-69385-0

THE HIGH COUNTRY RANCHER

Copyright © 2009 by M. Jan Hambright

PLEASE RECYCLE
THIS PRODUCT IS RECYCLABLE

Recycling programs
for this product may
not exist in your area.

www.eHarlequin.com

Printed in U.S.A.

U.S.: 3010 Walden Ave., P.O. Box 1325, Buffalo,
Canadian: P.O. Box 609, Fort Erie, Ont. L2A 5X3

ABOUT THE AUTHOR

Jan Hambright penned her first novel at seventeen, but claims it was pure rubbish. However, it did open the door on her love for storytelling. Born in Idaho, she resides there with her husband, three of their five children, a three-legged watch dog and a spoiled horse named Texas, who always has time to listen to her next story idea while they gallop along.

A self-described adrenaline junkie, Jan spent ten years as a volunteer EMT in rural Idaho, and jumped out of an airplane at ten-thousand feet attached to a man with a parachute, just to celebrate turning forty. Now she hopes to make your adrenaline level rise along with that of her danger-seeking characters. She would like to hear from her readers and hopes you enjoy the story world she has created for you. Jan can be reached at P.O. Box 2537, McCall, Idaho 83638.

Books by Jan Hambright

HARLEQUIN INTRIGUE
  865—RELENTLESS
  943—ON FIRE
  997—SHOWDOWN WITH THE SHERIFF
  1040—AROUND-THE-CLOCK PROTECTOR
  1118—THE HIGH COUNTRY RANCHER

Don't miss any of our special offers. Write to us at the following address for information on our newest releases.

Harlequin Reader Service
U.S.: 3010 Walden Ave., P.O. Box 1325, Buffalo, NY 14269
Canadian: P.O. Box 609, Fort Erie, Ont. L2A 5X3

CAST OF CHARACTERS

Baylor McCullough—After a past filled with too much pain, this rancher just wants to be left alone. Then a beautiful detective turns up injured on his ranch.

Detective Mariah Ellis—She's come to question Baylor McCullough about a missing local man. But thanks to a blizzard, she finds herself holed up on his property…and in his bed.

Prosecutor James Endicott—He's a missing person.

Amy McCullough—She's dead, but what pertinent information in this case died along with her?

Rachel Endicott—What's her connection to the case, other than knowing that Amy McCullough and her husband were having an affair?

Harley Neville—He's a nosey neighbor on the east side of the Bellwether ranch, but does he take nosey to an extreme?

Ryan Worchester—If there's evidence to be discovered, this CSI will uncover it.

Ray Buckner—He's a rodeo circuit cowboy with information. Will he live for his eight-second ride?

Chief Ted Ellis—Having a daughter who's a detective in his department makes him happy, but wonders if she'll be able to keep her objectivity where Baylor McCullough is concerned.

Travis Priestly—The ranch hand stumbled onto someone's secret and survived an attack, but will he come out of his coma in time to help?

Chapter One

Baylor McCullough flipped the collar of his oilskin duster up around his neck, and spurred his horse into the wind raging from the north in icy waves.

Snow pelted his face, stinging like tiny BBs, but he focused instead on the lay of the land, trying to define it in the blizzard swirling around him.

The warming pen in the barn brimmed with early spring calves, too young to survive the freak storm hammering the Salmon River high country.

Only one was missing. A bald-faced calf he'd seen with its mother yesterday afternoon before the sky clouded to murky white and the air temperature dipped below freezing.

Reining in his horse, Texas, he paused, spotting an outline in the snow just below the border of ancient ponderosa pines that lined the driveway leading into the ranch. The shape disappeared as the wind shifted, smearing his vision.

"Get up." He tapped his heels against the horse's

flanks and rocked forward in the saddle, aiming for the trees less than twenty yards away.

Night would fall soon; the storm was intensifying. Nothing would survive after dark. He was running out of time.

Texas's hooves thudded against the frozen earth as he searched for traction in the blowing snow and plowed through the drifts accumulating and dissipating like sand dunes on the Sahara.

Baylor forced his hat down hard on his head and steered the horse around a tangle of branches that had been ripped from one of the ponderosa. He'd be lucky if the storm didn't take out the power before it spent its fury on the Bellwether Ranch.

"Whoa." He eased back on the reins, stopped the horse and climbed down out of the saddle. Kneeling in the snow, he brushed hard, exposing the hide of the bald-faced calf he'd seen only yesterday, but he was too late.

He straightened. It was only one calf, only one in his herd of hundreds, but it was a loss. A knot clinched in the pit of his stomach. He mounted up, and turned Texas for the ranch a quarter of a mile away, fighting for every breath he dragged into his lungs from the blasting wind.

The pine branches he'd passed earlier whipped and jerked in the gale, like sheets on a clothesline.

Texas spooked and skittered sideways.

Baylor kept his seat in the saddle, bringing the scared horse under control.

For an instant the snow cleared, giving him a view he hadn't expected.

Concern slid through his veins, driving him forward. He bailed off his horse and went to the ground, digging into the snowdrift piled up against the limb, looking for the thing he believed he'd seen for a brief second, and praying he was wrong.

Brushing away the last of the snow, he stared down at a human hand.

He jerked off his leather glove and pressed his fingers to the wrist, feeling for a pulse. It drummed beneath his fingertips, faint and thready.

Still alive. But not for long if he didn't do something.

Baylor pushed to his feet and rushed to his horse.

Texas's eyes went wide. He took a couple of steps back.

"Easy boy." Hand out, Baylor touched the horse's neck, calming him, before he fumbled with the laces and untied his lariat from the saddle.

He trudged back through the snow and looped the noose of the rope around the thick base of the limb.

Striding back to his horse, he mounted up, wrapped the rope around the saddle horn and urged Texas back.

"Easy…easy." He coaxed, hoping to keep the spooked animal from an all-out bolt.

Three feet. Five feet. Ten feet. Clear.

Baylor dismounted, unwrapped the rope from the

saddle horn and coiled it up as he lunged back to the spot where the limb had fallen, trapping someone.

Dropping the rope, he went to his knees and started digging. Panic drove him, until he found the hand again. Reaching down, he judged where the body was and locked his arms around it. In one pull it came free, sending him backward onto his backside with his arms wrapped around a body, and a face full of snow, but it was the sight of a slender body, and a wisp of long blond hair sticking out from under a stocking cap that fisted worry in his gut.

A woman? A hypothermic woman, a dead woman, if he didn't get her back to the house. How long had she been lying there in the freezing cold? He mentally tried to establish a timeline as he stood up, and pulled her into his arms. She hadn't been there at 3:00 p.m. when he'd gone out to round up his cows and calves just before the storm broke.

Putting one foot in front of the other, he maneuvered through the snow until he reached Texas, who'd calmed and stood with his head low, hindquarters turned into the gale.

Gently, he draped her over the front of the saddle. Foot in stirrup, he mounted up and pulled her back into his arms, settling her against him.

Staring down, he saw her face for the first time. High cheekbones, a strong chin, full lips, refined, but much too still and void of color. The only thing marring her features was a bloody scrape on her right temple, probably caused by the limb when it hit her, knocked her down and trapped her.

Who was she? And what was she doing on the Bellwether?

Concern rattled through him. He might already be too late. He wasn't a doctor, but head injuries and hypothermia were serious business.

He turned Texas for home, hoping he had better luck saving the beautiful woman in his arms than he had had with the early spring calf who lay frozen to death in the snow.

DETECTIVE MARIAH ELLIS became aware of her body one tingling appendage at a time, starting with her toes. She was cold. As cold as she'd ever been, but the air against her bare skin was warm.

Her bare skin? A hazy image accompanied her return to consciousness: a man lying next to her, his body pressed to hers, his warmth soaking into her frozen veins.

In a burst of horror and disoriented thought, her eyelids shot open and she jerked upright in the bed. A bed she didn't recognize, in a room that didn't belong to her.

Covered with only a sheet, she grabbed the bulky rust-colored comforter folded at the foot of the massive four-poster, and yanked it up around her neck.

Quieting, she listened for any sound of movement. Her head throbbed, her stomach rebelling against the sudden jolt of excitement. Flopping back against the fluffy pillows, she waited for the nausea to pass.

The mournful howl of the wind blowing against the house was the only sound in the candlelit room, besides the crackle coming from a blazing fire burning in a massive stone fireplace, positioned against the wall opposite the bed.

Tension squeezed every muscle in her body as one-by-one she recovered her memories of the day's events.

She'd come to the Bellwether Ranch to question its owner, rancher Baylor McCullough, about a missing prosecutor, James Endicott.

Was this McCullough's home?

His bed?

Panic frayed her nerves and left her agitated.

She'd been advised to use caution where Baylor McCullough was concerned. He had been, after all, a suspect in his wife's death a year ago.

Scanning the room, she spotted the object of her search. Throwing back the comforter, she climbed out of bed. A chill raked over her bare skin and her gaze settled on a silky robe draped over the footboard.

Mariah swallowed, took two steps forward and snatched the garment. She pulled it on, securing the belt with a tight tug.

The room spun.

Grabbing for the footboard, she steadied herself.

Head pounding, she reached up and felt the gauze bandage taped in place on her right temple.

The branch. She'd been clipped by it while she'd walked along the road into the ranch after her car slid into the ditch half a mile back. Things were beginning to make sense. All but the faint memory of not being in the four-poster alone.

Had she dreamt that?

Taking several deep breaths, she focused on her service revolver and faltered forward until she reached the mirrored wooden dresser where it lay.

Wrapping her left hand around the holster, she pulled out the shiny .38 with her right, and instantly felt a surge of relief coat her nerves. A girl could always rely on her weapon.

She didn't know what Baylor McCullough was capable of, and she didn't want to find out. The .38 was the only deterrent between the two options, and she intended to use it if she had to.

Her feet stung as she turned around and stared at the open door that led out of the large bedroom. The flicker of candles in the adjacent darkness put her on edge.

Fighting the pain in her feet that resembled a zillion tiny needle pricks, she took a step forward, then another, shuffling until she reached the entry.

Stopping, she leaned against the doorjamb for support and scoped out what appeared to be the living room.

A fire blazed in a river-rock fireplace centered

against one wall. Light from the flames ebbed and flowed, touching the articles in the room with its glow.

Somewhere in the unfamiliar house Baylor McCullough waited.

Was he armed?

Raising her service revolver, she inched forward, getting a sense of the room's layout and analyzing it for cover.

The sound of someone's deep, even breathing sliced into her senses.

She turned toward the sound and stopped her advance.

She spotted the room's only occupant sprawled in a deep leather chair and focused on his denim-clad thighs, long, lean, well muscled and stretched out in front of him. His boot-encased feet were casually crossed at the ankles and rested on an ottoman.

By the time her tenuous gaze moved up his shirtless six-packed torso and settled on his face, she realized he was looking back.

"Detective Ellis." The surety in his voice rattled her nerves worse than any high-speed chase ever had.

With a force that took her breath away, she snapped back into the reality that belonged to her. She was a cop and he was her number one suspect, if she could find her badge, and her…clothes.

"And you'd be Baylor McCullough?"

He rocked forward in the chair, pushing the ottoman aside before he stood up, tall, broad-shouldered and silhouetted against the firelight.

Panic zipped along her nerve endings and her mouth went bone-dry.

"I believe you already know the answer, considering you found your way into my ranch."

Irritation warmed her insides as she lowered the pistol, her vulnerability exposed under his intense stare like a Norwegian tourist's winter skin on Maui in December.

Embarrassment fired in her body and hit its target on her cheeks. She wasn't a rookie; feeling like one bothered her.

"You…rescued me from the storm?"

He gave a tiny nod, confirming her suspicion and solidifying her troubles.

"My car slid into the ditch half a mile from here." She swallowed the lump in her throat, trying to salvage whatever thread of dignity she had left. She was bare-butt naked inside the silky robe, and she was sure he'd been the one who'd facilitated that little detail. This was no way to start an interview with a suspect, but it was the only starting point she had.

His chiseled features softened. His steel-blue eyes twinkled with amusement as he moved toward her in relaxed, even strides.

"I've got water on the cookstove. I'll make you some hot tea. You need to drink it."

"And my badge?"

The twinkle disappeared. His jaw, darkened by stubble, set in a hard line. He clamped his teeth together. "Hanging in the closet with your dry clothes."

A tingle raced through her body as she looked up at him, unsure if she should be cautious or apologetic. He had, after all, saved her life.

He must have sensed the quandary she found herself in because he attempted to smile. "This storm has us locked in. It'll be a couple of days before the outside world knows you're missing."

Mariah felt drained. The edges of her caution melted away for a moment only to be resolidified an instant later.

"I'll have to check for myself. Have you got a telephone I can use?"

"Out. Along with the electricity." He turned away from her and she stared at the well-developed muscles cording his back as he moved toward the kitchen.

"I'd stay off your feet for a day or two. You've got some frostbite. Walking around could damage the tissue, and you've got nice feet. Go back to bed if you want to keep your toes." With that warning and compliment he disappeared into the darkened kitchen just beyond the firelight.

Mariah's heart rate shot up. She'd managed to get herself into one heck of a mess. The idea of being trapped on a mountain with no phone, no car and a suspect with a foot fetish was more than she'd bargained for when she'd left the station this afternoon.

Still, she was glad he'd found her, because the alternative was a slow, cold death. She shivered, unsure if it was the result of the air temperature, or the idea of being held up with Baylor McCullough. Her prime suspect in the disappearance of James Endicott, the prosecutor who'd tried to charge him with vehicular manslaughter in his wife Amy's death.

Hobbling back to the bedroom, she clutched the .38 a little tighter.

BAYLOR PULLED A MUG out of the cupboard next to the sink and carried it over to the counter next to the cookstove. Every nerve in his body had twisted into a knot the moment he'd discovered her badge and gun in the process of removing her wet clothes.

He knew the lanky blonde with a kick-ass body who warmed his bed wasn't here to sell him a subscription to *Ladies' Home Journal.* So what did she want? He'd seen the way she gripped her pistol, picked up on the embarrassment of the situation she found herself in. Worse, she was afraid of him. That knowledge put his emotions in a tailspin. He'd never hurt a woman and he didn't plan to start now.

Opening a canister, he pulled out a tea bag, unwrapped it and put it in the cup, before filling it with hot water and setting the kettle back on the cookstove.

He dunked the tea bag, watching the liquid turn to amber in the candlelight before he removed it, squeezed it and laid it on the counter, trying to rid his mind of the body contact images branded on it.

He'd followed medical protocol for hypothermia. Right down to the skin-on-skin contact to rewarm her. He overrode a swell of desire that charged through him.

Detective Ellis was a beautiful woman, but now that he'd thawed her out, he had to keep her warm. Ice crystals in the bloodstream could cause cardiac arrest. The next several hours were critical.

Gradual rewarming was key, from the inside and out. But there was no way to tell how bad the bump on her head was. He had to watch over her until he could get her to the hospital in Grangeville sixty miles away.

He picked up the steaming mug and headed for the bedroom.

MARIAH SHOVED THE PISTOL under the pillow next to her and settled into bed, covering herself with the down comforter. She hated to admit Baylor McCullough was right. She'd had enough first-aid training to know walking around on frozen feet could result in losing toes. She jiggled her legs, trying to aid circulation.

The clop of boots on hardwood brought her gaze up. He entered the room with a steaming mug in hand.

Her pulse kicked up a notch. She tried to crush the instant attraction that sizzled through her, by remembering why she was here, but it didn't work.

She was a cop, not blind, and Baylor McCullough was an attractive man, from his intense blue-gray eyes, to his dark good looks and muscular build.

At any other time in her life, she might have explored her reaction to him, but she was here in an official capacity. The only thing that would have made her feel better was being dressed, instead of tied up in a slinky robe that had probably belonged to Amy McCullough, a dead woman.

"How are your feet?"

Damn…damn…damn, she thought, as she stared up at him, her gaze locked with his. There was that foot thing again.

"They feel like the only pincushion at a ladies' quilt club on a Monday afternoon."

"You should have stayed down." He set the cup on the nightstand and retreated to the foot of the bed.

Before she could utter an objection, he pulled the comforter back and exposed her feet.

Mariah braced herself when he touched her right foot, taking it in both hands.

She was unprepared for her body's response to his gentle touch, or the desire that flared and twisted through her, taking her breath with it. She closed her eyes, hoping he hadn't gotten a read on her, but the moment she opened them again, she knew that wish was futile.

His eyes narrowed, a half smile pulling at the left side of his sexy mouth. "Better?" he asked.

Mariah cleared her throat and focused on the sensation. The needling was slowly beginning to relent. She wiggled her toes trying to ignore the feel of his warm hands firmly forcing the blood to the surface of her skin with each stroke.

"It's not too bad. I can feel my toes."

"We caught it in time, but you need to stay off them." He put her right foot down and started on the left. By now she'd gotten used to his hands on her skin and she tried to relax. Tried to make it a clinical experience even though her body was humming and aware of his every movement.

"You've dealt with frostbite a time or two?"

"Living this far from civilization, it's a necessary skill."

"One I'm glad you possess." Warmth worked its way up her lower legs. "Thank you for rescuing me, and my toes."

"You're welcome." He settled her foot onto the bed and pulled the covers back over her feet.

"I'd like to know what you're doing on my ranch, Detective Ellis."

Mariah bristled at the abrupt change of subject. "I'm here to ask you a few questions."

He didn't speak. She pushed on. "Were you aware James Endicott went missing two weeks ago?" She considered herself an expert on suspect behavior and body language; she planned to absorb even the slightest measure of reaction he exhibited.

His blue eyes glistened with anger. A muscle pulsed along his square jawline, and his breathing rate shot up.

Mariah's heart skipped a beat as she visualized the

pistol tucked under the pillow next to her, ready to be used if he showed any sign of aggression toward her.

He knew something; he had to. His dislike for the man was obvious from his physical reaction.

"And you believe I had something to do with it? Once a suspect, always a suspect?" A glimmer of amusement flashed in his eyes and played out of sync with the seriousness of the implication.

"He tried to put you behind bars, Mr. McCullough. That's motive."

"For the record, Detective, he has tried to put hundreds behind bars. Many more badass than me."

She knew it was true, but she planned to push him. Interesting things bubbled out of people when you stressed them beyond their capacity to withhold the truth.

"I'll give you that one, but we're not talking about those badasses. We're talking about you. You've got to have some resentment built up. You've had almost a year to plan your revenge."

His face went placid, hiding the emotions she knew rippled just under the surface and beyond her reach for the moment.

"I've had time to figure things out. Time to make sense of what happened to Amy. A patch of hell, Detective, not a minute of it spent on revenge."

He stood at the foot of the bed looking like a warrior poised for battle. Hard, prepared, invincible.

Mariah suppressed an insurmountable wave of sympathy. "Will you consent to a polygraph?"

Clutching the footboard rail, he stared at her for a moment before she saw his shoulders relax. Whatever grudge existed between the two men was still there. She had the facts of the case, but not from his point of view.

"No." His arms dropped to his sides. "Get some rest." He strode out of the room, leaving her alone with a crackling fire and more questions than answers.

Gingerly she picked up the steaming mug he'd carried in, and smelled the vapors. Earl Grey, her favorite. Its rich aroma of bergamot wafted up her nose and calmed her nerves. She clutched the mug in both hands, letting the blessed warmth infuse her fingers.

She was lucky to be alive. She owed Baylor McCullough her life. Could she cut him some slack?

The question burned a path in her brain between her professional obligation as an officer of the law, and her happiness at being alive instead of a human popsicle.

She sipped the tea, letting it heat her throat, until she was warm and relaxed and barely able to keep her eyelids open. Setting the empty mug on the nightstand, she snuggled into the covers, listening to the wind batter the sturdy ranch house, much like her gratitude toward Baylor McCullough battered her resolve about his guilt.

Amy McCullough had been her friend years ago, but she'd lost touch with her after high school. How had she and Baylor met? What had their relationship been like?

She closed her eyes, letting the questions compile in her brain. She'd read every last word of the accident report, every interview…so why had James Endicott been so determined to prosecute Baylor in a case that read like a tragic accident out of a horror flick?

Chapter Two

Wham…wham…wham.

Mariah bolted awake and sat up, trying to place the loud banging coming from somewhere in the unfamiliar house.

A fire still blazed in the fireplace. Fresh wood had recently been added, judging by the still uncharred ends of the logs.

"Hello," she called out. No response.

Where was Baylor?

A measure of caution edged down her spine. She threw back the covers and crept out of bed.

"Hello," she called as she crossed to the doorway and stared out into the living room.

The fire in the living-room hearth was little more than a heap of glowing embers now, but Baylor's woodsy scent hung in the air, surrounding her, and she sensed he hadn't been gone long.

Wham!

Mariah jumped.

A cut of icy wind sliced into her, raising goose bumps on her body. The noise was coming from somewhere in the area of the kitchen.

Easing forward, she searched the darkness, heading toward the sound.

Wham!

Through the mudroom adjacent to the kitchen, she spotted the source of the racket and stalked toward it.

The back door stood wide-open before another gust of wind caught it and slammed it against the jamb.

A shudder coursed through her as she stepped out onto the porch and grabbed the knob. She paused in place, staring out into the darkness.

The storm had passed while she'd slept. A full moon gleamed against the platinum snow and bathed the landscape in brilliant white light. Somewhere in the surrounding woods a series of howls built to a mournful crescendo and echoed against the mountains. She half expected to see a wolf silhouette itself against the moon, and the stark beauty of the place, along with its mystery, appealed to her artist's eye.

But where was Baylor McCullough?

Stepping back, she pulled the door shut, but it wouldn't latch. She jiggled the knob back and forth. The bolt released. She pulled it shut again, and heard the cylinder pop into the kick plate.

Taking one last glance through the small panel of windows in the door, she saw a trail of movement.

In the timberline a hundred yards from the house, someone waded through the snow, before vanishing out of sight in the dense line of trees.

Was it McCullough? What was he doing out there? She turned the dead bolt and heard it lock in place.

"Detective?"

She jerked around, instinct taking over. Every muscle in her body coiled for maximum self-preservation. She lashed out at the man standing too close to her, catching him in the jaw with an upper-cut from her elbow before she realized she'd just hit Baylor in the face.

"Oh, shoot, I'm sorry. I thought you were out-side." She glanced back to the spot where she'd seen someone only an instant ago.

"I've been in the barn, checking on the calves." Baylor rubbed the spot on his jaw where she'd popped him. "I use the front door. I keep this one locked until I can get a locksmith up here to fix it. It doesn't always latch."

"I saw someone, up there, just at the timberline." She pointed to the spot. "Were you up there?"

"No. You probably saw deer feeding by the moonlight." He moved in next to her and stared out the window.

"Do deer walk upright?" she asked, half joking, but Baylor's features in the lunar glow were dead serious.

"Some strange things have been going on around here the past few months."

His cautious tone fired her curiosity. "What sort of things?"

Baylor reached for her hand and turned her toward the living room. He could feel the cold in the air through his heavy coat, and he knew she had to be freezing in the little black robe.

"It's not important." He felt her shiver, the vibration rippling through his hand. He coaxed her a little faster toward the bedroom and the heat from the fireplace.

"It's almost dawn. You have to stay warm." He ushered her through the doorway into the bedroom and released her, not content until she climbed back into bed, and pulled the covers up around her neck.

He took off his coat, picked up the poker, opened the fireplace screen and jostled the logs. A spray of sparks jumped, and the fire hissed as it intensified.

There was that feeling again, but this time there was something solid to back it up.

The hair on the back of his neck bristled as firelight danced across the hardwood floor of the bedroom and reflected in a set of liquid footprints. The spot where someone had stood long enough for the snow on their shoes to melt. Someone had been in this room tonight while Mariah slept, and the prints didn't belong to him.

"What woke you up?" He slid the screen closed and sat down on the hearth. He didn't want to spook her. She'd go cop on him again.

"The back door was wide-open and banging against the doorjamb in the wind."

Could the figure she'd seen outside be the person who made the tracks in the corner? He didn't know, but he wouldn't relax until he got her safely off the mountain.

"Get some rest." He moved into the chair next to the fireplace, to stand guard, and watched her close her beautiful blue eyes.

Whatever was going on at the Bellwether Ranch was his problem, and he didn't want her involved.

THE SMELL OF COFFEE brewing and bacon sizzling pulled Mariah out of sleep. She opened her eyes, staring at the lamp on the nightstand, at the lit bulb that glared from under the shade. The power was back on.

She rolled onto her back, staring up at the coffered ceiling. She could hear pearls of water dripping outside the bedroom window as sunlight penetrated the slats in the wooden blinds.

Idaho weather was so unpredictable—if you didn't like it, wait five minutes and it would change.

Throwing back the covers, she climbed out of bed and stretched. Her body ached, every muscle had gone stiff. Probably a by-product of nearly freezing to death, she decided as she went to the closet and opened it to find her clothes hanging just where Baylor said they'd be.

She dressed quickly, strapped on her service revolver, and made the bed up in the decidedly masculine room that carried his scent.

She headed for the kitchen, taking her time as she surveyed the living room in the light of day. Heavy hand-hewn beams crossed the ceiling. The hardwood floor under her feet was made of maple, and polished to perfection. Amy had great taste, she decided as she turned toward the kitchen, her gaze locking on Baylor.

He worked over the stove, his broad shoulders covered in a pristine white T-shirt. Every little nagging ounce of desire in her body fizzed up, and she had to look away.

"Good morning," he said as he turned around. "How do you feel?"

Pulling out a stool at the bar, she slid onto it and fixed a smile on her face. "Great."

He turned to a cupboard next to the sink, pulled down a large red coffee mug and filled it from the coffeemaker. "This should help."

A grin pulled his lips apart, showing even, white teeth. Her heart did a somersault. He set the cup in front of her. "Do you take anything in it?"

"Black's fine." Picking up the cup, she took a swallow, wondering if he'd been as attentive toward Amy. There it was again, that curiosity about something she didn't need to know. Something that had no bearing on her investigation into James Endicott's disappearance.

Baylor could feel her eyes on his back like a tick on a horse, but at least she'd left her gun holstered this morning instead of pointed at him.

"I called a tow truck for your car. He'll be here within the hour." He said all this over his shoulder as he loaded her plate with scrambled eggs, bacon and a slice of wheat toast.

"I'm going to take you up to the hospital. Make sure you're all right."

"That's not necessary. I can take care of myself."

He didn't doubt it. His jaw still hurt. He slid the plate in front of her and took his first long look at her in broad daylight.

Her tousled blond hair was loose, and fell to her shoulders in soft curls that made his hands ache to touch them. She wasn't tall, but she wasn't short. And those eyes, the ones flashing him a back-off warning as sure as he was standing there, well, he liked those, too. The color of a cloudless noonday sky.

"My rules. You got hurt on my property, I've got an obligation to make sure you check out."

Her mouth dropped open, but she shut it, picked up a piece of bacon and took a bite.

He turned around, satisfied that she'd be safe for the next two hours. He couldn't risk having her wandering around on his mountain alone. This morning he'd found a set of footprints in the melting snow next to the timberline, right where the good detective said she saw someone last night.

Whatever was going on didn't involve her, and he wasn't about to let anything happen to her.

Detective Mariah Ellis was better off back where she belonged. Far away from the Bellwether Ranch.

MARIAH SLID INTO THE cab of Baylor's black Chevy pickup and buckled up. What was left of last night's snowstorm lay in melting drifts, and the sun was warm against her face.

He fired up the truck and backed out of the driveway.

She tried to relax, but it was impossible. She'd yet to accomplish what she'd set out to do. Interrogate Baylor McCullough.

"I'd like you to come into the station for an interview. I need to know where you were on April the fifth." She glanced at the muddy road in front of them, before slipping him a glance.

His jaw was set; he stared straight ahead. She knew defiance when she saw it.

"If you had nothing to do with Endicott's disappearance, you're in the clear." The word *but* hung up on her tongue. She was so sure he was somehow involved when she'd come tearing up the mountain yesterday afternoon. Now she wasn't as convinced, but she still had a job to do.

"A polygraph could clear you."

His knuckles whitened on the steering wheel. "You're going to need a lot more than a hunch, Detective."

A chill launched over her skin and landed in her gut. He was right. She was reaching. But a reach was all she had to go on at the moment. He was her only lead.

"If that's the way you want to play it for the time being, but it's the surest way to clear yourself."

Baylor didn't doubt it. It was the principle of the whole damn thing. His past was playing into it, he was sure. In the eyes of the law he'd always be suspect.

He rounded the bend in the road and spotted the tow truck along with another pickup parked in the opposite direction. He slowed and pulled in behind it.

The tow-truck driver raised his hand and waved. The man standing next to him did the same and Baylor recognized his neighbor Harley Neville who lived a mile up the road.

"You can stay in the truck and keep warm if you like." He pulled the handle and the door swung open. He somehow doubted she'd take that option. Mariah Ellis likely lived on curiosity and adrenaline. Both went with her line of work.

"I'd like to have a look." She climbed out of the truck and moved up next to him as he covered ground in long, even strides.

Her late model Ford Taurus was augered deep in the ditch. The rear end sticking up in the air, the undercarriage high-centered on the berm of earth, the nose rammed into the embankment.

"Bang-up job." A whistle hissed from between

his lips, drawing a glare from her that could have cut diamonds.

He stared down the road, taking note of the exact spot where she'd gotten sideways, where she'd made the mistake of hitting her brakes, and where she'd ended up. Lucky she hadn't been seriously hurt, or he wouldn't have found her in time to save her life.

"This your car?" the tow-truck driver asked, shifting his green Bernie's Garage hat off then back on, before settling it low on his forehead.

"Yeah. It's mine. You can send the bill to the county sheriff's department."

"Will do." He moved to his wrecker and unhooked the wench cable.

"Harley, how are you?" Baylor asked, shaking the other man's hand.

"Not too shabby. The little lady was lucky this happened here and not a few miles back."

Baylor glanced over at Mariah, who shaded her eyes against the sun beating down on them, making it almost impossible to believe only last night the area had been covered in six inches of fresh snow.

Harley was right. Less than two miles west where the river ran straight and the road turned south, there would have been nothing to keep the car from plunging over the edge into the river below.

He sobered and shook off the blanket of dread that suddenly covered him, making his chest feel tight and his mouth go dry.

"Looks like Bernie has this. Let's head for Grangeville."

Mariah nodded and turned toward the truck. He exchanged a nod with Harley and followed her back to the rig, enjoying the sway of her hips in her dark blue slacks. If he had to have a cop on his doorstep and in his bed, he wanted her.

They got into the pickup and pulled out around Harley's shiny new rig. It must have cost him a small fortune, Baylor decided as he eased past the tow truck and picked up speed.

"How long have you been on the ranch?" she asked, casting a glance his way before leaning forward in the seat to study the landscape flitting past on the right.

"I took over the Bellwether from my folks in 1998. My dad's health wasn't so good and he couldn't take the winters up here anymore. Now they have a place in Arizona."

"There's something to be said for staying warm."

"What about your parents?" He braked and made the wide sweeping turn that put them parallel to the river a hundred feet below.

"Divorced. My dad lives in Grangeville, my mom in Lewiston."

Damn. Why hadn't he made the connection sooner? A thread of apprehension laced through him, knotting his muscles. "Ted Ellis is your dad?"

"That's right."

The knots didn't loosen, and the knowledge put him on alert. Her father was the chief of police. He'd worked damn hard to follow the law, not engage it in spades. Now there were two Ellises who had it in for him.

Thump!

The truck jerked hard to the right and veered close to the edge of the riverbank.

A shriek escaped from between Mariah's lips.

"Hang on!" Baylor pulled left on the steering wheel.

Thump! The truck jerked again, sending them into the opposite lane.

Baylor pulled it back and pushed down hard on the brakes. The pickup ground to a stop in the middle of the muddy road.

Mariah's hand was on the door handle and she was out of the truck before he could assure her they were fine, but he doubted she'd have much to do with the notion, considering all the color had drained from her face.

He hopped out and came around the front of the rig to stare at the problem.

One lug nut was the lone survivor holding on to the right front tire.

Caution worked his nerves, and he touched Mariah's back, feeling the tension in her body.

"Someone wanted you to have an accident. Someone did this on purpose. Those don't just fall off."

She had a point, but he didn't want to tell her this was the second time in the past month his pickup had been sabotaged. He moved for the rear of the truck to get his toolbox and a lug wrench.

He'd get her off his mountain and safely back to town even if he had to carry her there himself.

DR. JEROME MUNSEY shined a narrow beam of light into her right eye, then her left, before he stepped back to the counter, laid the scope down and prepared a dressing to cover the scrape on her right temple.

"You've got a mild concussion, Mariah, but no permanent damage. You should be fine." He moved in next to where she sat on the end of the examining table and put the dressing on her wound.

"Baylor got to you before there was any damage to the soft tissues of your appendages. You were lucky." He stepped back and put his hands in the pockets of his blue lab coat. "Call me if you experience any dizziness, or nausea. Numbness or tingling in your hands and feet."

"Okay." She slipped her socks back on, head down as she tried to cover the mix of horror and embarrassment that pulsed in every cell of her body. The trip to the E.R. had confirmed her suspicions. Baylor had, in fact, rewarmed her with skin-on-skin contact. That hazy image was no dream. It was a reality that would be forever burned into her brain. Just the thought sent her imagination off on a tangent. What was worse was the way it made her feel, all hot and bothered.

She slid Baylor a quick glance. "I'm sure it was tough for him to handle, but it worked. Here I am, good as new." She hopped off the examining table and shoved her feet into her shoes. The sooner she got home the better. She wasn't sure she could handle another minute with him, now that she knew the full extent of what had transpired between them.

He was a suspect in a missing persons case; she had to focus on that, rather than the heat of the sexual tension that jumped between them like an unchecked forest fire.

Smiling at Dr. Munsey, she thanked him and left the E.R., headed for the exit.

"Take it easy, Detective." The sorry-about-that note in Baylor's voice pulled her up short.

"You should have told me!" She felt her cheeks flame, hot and telltale. "I know you did what you had to, but it's so…"

"Intimate?"

"Yes!" And unprofessional, she thought as she pushed through the main entrance door of the hospital and out onto the sidewalk, aiming for Baylor's pickup parked at the curb, while she tried to pull herself together.

Baylor stared at Mariah's backside. "Look." He reached for her shoulder and stopped her before she could get into the truck.

She turned on him, her anger visible in the rigid set of her jaw. Her blue eyes all but sparked.

"Would it help if I told you it was clinical? I was more interested in saving your life than exploring your body." He wrestled with a rush of desire that closed his throat.

She gave him a wary stare as he reached for the door handle and opened it for her. "Let's get you home."

He closed the door behind her, went around to the driver's side and climbed in. "Where to?"

"I live at 405 Cottonwood. It's off Sycamore on the west side of town."

"I know the street." He fired the engine and pulled out onto Main, searching for the right words. Why was she so upset? He wasn't sorry for saving her life; hell, he'd probably done himself a favor, but there had to be more to it. He'd never take advantage of a woman, especially one who was borderline coma-tose and not in control of her faculties.

Realization slammed into his brain. He opened his mouth to speak, then closed it. Mariah Ellis had a boyfriend? Explaining what had happened to her and how he'd saved her was going to complicate her life.

"No one besides Doc Munsey and you and I have to know what happened. I'm willing to let it go unsaid if it'll keep the peace between you and your...boyfriend." He flipped on his blinker and turned right onto Sycamore Street.

"Thanks for that," she whispered. "He'll be thrilled."

Mariah nibbled at her lower lip and stared out at the familiar street. It seemed like an eon since she'd last driven down it. So when in that short span of time had she left her straight-talking style twisting in the wind? She should just tell him she didn't have a boyfriend. There was no one in her life; her job had taken care of that.

"There. The yellow house on the left." She pointed it out and tried to relax. Cop. She was a cop, she needed to start acting like one, even if she didn't feel the vibe and hadn't for a long time. She still had a major case to solve. Baylor rolled to a stop in front of the yellow house, with a white picket fence and massive pots brimming with pink flowers on either side of the front steps.

He couldn't shake the disappointment of knowing she had someone in her life. Hell, he was happy for her. She was a beautiful woman. He gritted his teeth and climbed out of the pickup, meeting her on the sidewalk before opening the gate and following her up the walk.

She stopped, fished in her pocket and pulled out a house key. "Come in for a drink before you head back."

His first response was to pass, but he didn't; instead, he followed her inside and watched as she shuffled into the kitchen. "Is sun tea okay?"

"Yeah." Baylor gazed around the living room. The place was neat and appointed with cushy furniture.

Her scent tinged the air, a mix of sweet and spicy. His gaze held on a piece of landscape artwork on the wall behind her beige sofa. Moving closer, he focused on the artist's signature in the bottom right corner. Mariah Ellis.

"This is your work," he said as she came into the living room with a glass of iced tea in each hand.

"Recognize the setting?" She smiled and he realized how relaxed she looked for the first time since he'd met her.

"The Seven Devils Mountain Range…from the Pappoose Creek side."

"Very good." She handed him the cold glass. "Do you want to see more?"

There was a note of excitement in her voice. Her eyes took on a sparkle he hadn't noticed before. This was Mariah Ellis's passion. This was what made her tick. Her art.

Moving down the hall, she showed him paintings of Mirror Lake, the Salmon River Canyon and a moose standing knee-deep in a pond at dawn feeding on moss.

"You should open a gallery. Your work is very good."

She warmed under his praise and his breath caught in his lungs. There was something innocent about her, something as unspoiled as her art, and he wanted to kiss her in the worst way, but he reined in the urge. He'd probably get the other side of his jaw popped. Didn't she already think he'd stepped over the line when he rewarmed her? How would she explain a kiss to her boyfriend? Frozen lips?

He took a deep gulp from his glass and turned toward the living room and escape. He'd fulfilled his obligation. She was home safe.

"Thanks for the drink." He handed the glass to her at the door and glanced down at an open book lying on a small table.

His heart jumped in his chest. He reached out and picked up the high-school yearbook.

Staring up at him from the page was a picture of Mariah and Amy. Arms locked, leaning against a set of lockers. The caption read, "Friends Forever."

His gut squeezed. He looked at Mariah. "You knew my wife, Amy?"

"We were best friends our sophomore year of high school."

A wave of caution raced through him, leaving him cold inside where he'd been warm only moments ago.

This was personal. Her suspicions about his involvement in Endicott's disappearance were fueled by her certainty about his guilt in Amy's death. There would never be an end to it. He'd done everything he could to save her life that night, short of drowning himself.

He closed the book and put it down. "I've got a long drive back to the ranch." He turned the doorknob and pulled the door open.

"Baylor."

He paused without turning around.

"For what it's worth, thank you."

"You're welcome." He didn't look back, just stepped out and pulled the door shut behind him.

He'd see her again. He knew it. Come Monday morning she'd have her cop face on, and he'd have to prove himself all over again.

Chapter Three

"You've got some explaining to do."

Young lady. Mariah mentally finished the sentence she'd outgrown a long time ago and closed her father's office door to keep the gossip to a minimum. Everyone in the department seemed to already know she'd spent Friday night trapped on a mountain with a suspect. She had no idea how things got spread, but they did, like butter on a waffle.

"I told you my car went into the ditch in the storm. The electricity and phone lines were down. I had no cell service up there, and no way out. If Baylor McCullough hadn't found me, you'd be hanging at the morgue right now identifying my frozen remains, so give it a rest."

Chief Ellis's mouth opened, then closed as he rocked back in his chair, and studied his daughter. "Do you still think he had something to do with Endicott's disappearance?"

Mariah swallowed, digging for her feelings on

a matter she'd been so sure of only days ago. Baylor's guilt.

"I don't know. But he's hiding something. You should have seen his reaction when I spoke about Endicott. There's definitely some animosity there."

"Hell, yeah. Endicott pressed him to the wall. I never understood exactly why he went after him so hard. The evidence seemed to support Amy McCullough's death as a tragic accident. But enough rage to snatch the man and make him go away? You got anyone else on the list?"

"I accounted for everyone Endicott prosecuted. They're either walking a straight line, out-of-state, dead or back in custody. McCullough is the only one who still lives around here."

"You're lucky he doesn't file a harassment suit against you. Make sure you play him straight. If he is involved, we need a clean case, no loopholes he could slip through."

"Okay." She stood up to leave, her nerves as tense as a race car driver's waiting at the start line.

There was only one way to capitalize on her suspicion. She'd have to stake out the Bellwether Ranch. If she could find probable cause, she could get a search warrant. Maybe she could find what he was hiding. She just hoped it wasn't Endicott.

BAYLOR MOVED PAST THE kitchen window for the third time in ten minutes, making sure he saw what he saw. He raised the binoculars to his eyes and adjusted the focus, dialing in the nose of the vehicle parked west of the ranch in a patch of trees a quarter of a mile away.

Detective Ellis's white car. She'd been there since dawn. Watching, waiting for him to make a move. Amusement rippled through him. He put the field glasses down.

If determination was all it took to be a cop, she would take the prize. Too bad she was so far off target. Granted, he hated what Endicott had done to him and the effect it had on his life, but he had nothing to do with his disappearance.

Baylor headed outside to the barn. Somehow convincing Detective Ellis of that fact seemed important. If she wanted evidence, he'd show her there wasn't any, not on the Bellwether Ranch anyway.

MARIAH CLOSED HER EYES for an instant, trying to stop them from burning. She'd been on the stakeout since five this morning, and her coffee thermos was empty.

This had to be one of the worst ideas she'd ever managed to employ, at least on a twenty-five-hundred-acre ranch. Baylor could have hidden Endicott anywhere. Maybe she should give it up and go back to square one. Good, old-fashioned, pound-the-pavement, last-person-to-see-him-alive kind of stuff. Someone had to have seen something. She just had to pose the right question to the right person.

She opened her eyes and was startled. The object of her crack-of-dawn investigation stood next to her car holding the reins to a couple of horses.

"Good morning," he said. "You'll never get any nosing around done sitting in your car."

Damn, she'd been caught. "You have a better plan?"

"How about I give you a tour of the ranch on horseback. You can search for Endicott anywhere you'd like."

"And if I find him?" The air inside the vehicle went hot.

"You can cuff me and take me to jail."

"Deal." She rolled up the driver's-side window, climbed out of the car and locked it. "I haven't ridden in a while. Is he gentle?"

"Jericho? Yeah. The last person he dumped lived to tell about it."

She grinned, feeling like a 4-H student at her first horse show.

Baylor handed her the reins, watched her mount up and settle into the saddle. He could only hope that his method worked. That the beautiful detective would drive away happy and convinced there wasn't a body hidden somewhere on the Bellwether.

"We'll head east. That's the most remote area of the ranch. Lots of game trails. Abandoned mine shafts. I don't run cattle out there for that reason."

"Too dangerous?"

"One wrong step and you don't come home." He

turned his horse and headed for the main road. They'd follow it for a couple of miles and take the Bear Creek trailhead just before Harley Neville's place.

Mariah nudged her horse up next to Baylor's and tried to relax. The feel of her sidearm on her belt offered some comfort. Searching without a search warrant, riding next to a suspect, all seemed a little strange to her, but if it helped her pull together a case, it'd be worth the risk.

"Shoot. I forgot my lunch in the car." She attempted to turn the horse back toward her vehicle.

"Don't worry." Baylor patted his saddlebag. "I brought enough for two." He grinned and her heartbeat went haywire.

Maybe this wasn't such a good idea. Her certainty about his involvement in Endicott's disappearance seemed to flail whenever she was with him. Something about his easygoing style sucked her in and changed her mind.

Baylor spurred his horse and she followed suit as they settled into a slow canter that ate up the distance.

The sweet scent of honey locust and pine sap hung in the air. The rhythm of the horses' hooves against the dirt lulled her into a contented state that she'd rarely achieved since she'd started working at the sheriff's department.

Baylor reined his horse in and waited for her to do the same. "Here's our trail. It's a steep climb, but the view on top is worth it."

There was that sensation again. That zing of pleasure across her nerves, that flutter in her chest. "Looks like it would be too much work to get a body up there." She stared up the sloping trail as it disappeared into the trees.

Her comment put an edge of tension in the air between them, which was precisely what she needed to pull her back down to earth. Until the Endicott case was solved, and Baylor was cleared, she had to sock the odd feelings away somewhere so they didn't interfere with her job.

"A good strong horse and some determination. It could be done," he said without hesitation.

She stared at him, trying to gauge his emotions, but his face gave nothing away. Was he joking or dead serious, she couldn't be sure.

"Let's head up. Make sure it's clear." He tipped his hat, the one shielding his features from her scrutiny.

She fell in behind him, leaning forward in the saddle as her horse trudged up the first steep incline, then took a right as the trail switched back across the face of the mountain.

Half an hour later they reined in their horses under a massive ponderosa pine and dismounted.

Mariah's legs were shaking as she got them underneath her and took a look around. Breathtaking vistas spread out in front of her everywhere she turned.

"What do you think?" Baylor asked, tying the horses to a low-hanging limb.

"It's beautiful." Already her artist's eye was honing in on all the possible angles she could use in her work. "I could stay up here for days and have something new to capture on every one of them."

"I knew you'd like it." He untied the double-pouched saddlebag, pulled it off the back of the saddle and tossed it over his shoulder. "Come on, there's a place to relax just up the trail."

Mariah tagged along behind him, staring at his broad shoulders as they moved beneath his denim shirt. Every ounce of control she possessed seemed to drain away, and desire, intense and volatile, throbbed in her veins.

She swallowed, focusing on the trail ahead of them as it opened into a small meadow flanked by dense timber. A gushing creek roared from out of the mountainside, then slowed and meandered across the meadow before dumping into a pond.

A well-traveled path wound through the heart of the clearing, flanked by knee-deep bear grass, ending next to a sandy beach on the banks of the pond.

"This is perfect." She attempted to move past him, determined to sort out all the unfamiliar emotions tangled up inside of her, but he reached out and caught her hand, pulling her toward him.

A jolt of electricity coursed through her as they

made contact. Gazing up into his face, she knew he'd felt it, too.

"Mariah…I…" What the hell was he thinking? Baylor wondered as he stared at her lips, then back into her eyes. He was a man on fire. He'd wanted to kiss her all morning and hadn't been able to shake the desire. He'd even tried to remind himself she was a cop, out for blood, and still it hadn't done the trick.

He pulled off his cowboy hat, gave it a toss and dropped the saddlebags as he lowered his mouth to hers. She didn't resist. Instead, her arms came up around his neck.

Mariah's head swam. Every nerve in her body attuned itself to the feel of Baylor's body pressed against hers.

She opened her mouth for him, tasting him as he deepened the kiss, exploring her with his tongue in a slow, sensual rhythm. An ache manifested itself deep and low in her belly. A primal need that begged for satisfaction as he lowered her to the soft meadow grass.

Fire ignited in her veins, consuming all reasonable thought in its flame. She wasn't a cop, he wasn't her suspect. They were a man and a woman, locked in the heat of desire. Lost in their own private heaven. Oblivious to the world around them.

The first bullet whizzed past Baylor's right ear and bored into the ground next to his head, sending up a spray of dirt.

Somewhere in the timberline on the other side of the meadow, the gunshot echoed back.

Drunk on desire, Baylor rocked back, staring down at her. Reality jolted him into action. Someone was shooting at them.

He rolled them both hard to the left, took her hand and dragged her to her feet.

"Run!" he yelled.

Ping.

Another bullet zinged past, hitting the ground inches behind them.

Baylor aimed for the trees two hundred feet in front of them, caution driving him as he tried to pick the safest place to go off trail. The meadow was riddled with boarded-over vertical mine shafts; one wrong step and…

Before the thought had time to solidify, the earth gave under his feet.

In a last desperate attempt to save Mariah, he yanked hard, sending her flying past him, but the cavernous hole was too big.

It swallowed them whole and they fell through the rotting boards into darkness.

Mariah hit the bottom of the pit with a thud. The air pushed from her lungs as she slammed into the ground. Pain shot through her body from the jarring drop.

Baylor hit next to her.

She heard him grunt.

Dust clogged her mouth and nose, grit showering her tongue and grating on her teeth.

She lay still and opened her eyes.

It was dark at the bottom of the hole, and it took a moment for them to adjust. She scanned the earthen walls of the mine shaft. They were trapped.

She choked back a sob, drawing on her training instead. A cool head was the best tool in a situation like this.

"Baylor, can you hear me?" she asked, encouraged by a scraping noise and a grunt.

"Yeah."

The sound of his voice sent a charge of excitement through her. He was alive.

"How deep do you suppose this shaft is?"

"Thirty feet maybe."

May as well be a hundred, she thought as she pulled herself up into a sitting position, looking for anything that could help them escape.

"Are you hurt?"

"Does my pride count?"

She smiled in the darkness. "No."

"Good."

Mariah pulled herself to her feet, dusting off the layer of dirt that coated her body. She watched Baylor stand up, testing his feet under him before he put his head back and gazed up at the beams of light pouring through the jagged slats of wood above their heads.

The shaft was tight, maybe six by six.

A chill rocked her body and she fought a wave of hopelessness. They had to find a way out or this hole would become their grave.

Baylor wiped a trickle of blood off his forehead with the back of his hand and stared up at the opening.

The walls of the vertical shaft were laced with tree roots, the only thing that had slowed their fall. Worry hammered through him, pounding his nerves to a pulp. In frustration he grabbed a root and tested it for stability, but after a hard jerk it pulled out of the wall, coating him in more dirt.

"Dammit." He sucked in a breath and focused on Mariah, who stood still, her head cocked at an odd angle.

"Do you hear that?"

"Hear what?"

"A horse."

Baylor listened, hearing nothing at first, then in the distance the thud of horse hooves against the earth. More than one horse. Their horses, he guessed.

Caution exploded inside of him and he pulled Mariah into his arms, moving her back against the wall of the shaft. "Shh," he whispered against her ear, as a shadow fell across the opening of the hole, blocking the sunlight for an instant.

First his hat landed at their feet, popping up a ring of dust, then the saddlebags followed, dropping at his feet with a thud.

His pulse began to hammer in his ears. Whoever had taken shots at them didn't want there to be any evidence left aboveground. Nothing to indicate they'd ever been in the meadow. Baylor held Mariah closer. Would the shooter stare into the hole? Would he pick them off with his rifle one after the other like caged animals with nowhere to run?

The sickening clank of a board dropping into place set Baylor's nerves on end.

The shaft of light streaming into the hole from above narrowed. Then another board and another were laid over the top until the opening was covered.

He felt Mariah shudder, and stroked her hair. "Hold on," he whispered, attempting to calm her. They had to stay quiet; they had to let him believe they were dead, or close to it. They didn't stand a chance of surviving if he opened fire on them in the hole.

Baylor waited, counting the minutes, then the hour, before he let go of her and dropped to his knees, searching for his saddlebags in the darkness. He locked his hands on them and fumbled inside, pulling out the flashlight he always carried. He switched it on, and their prison became illuminated.

"It's probably safe to talk." He shined the light up at the opening, covered over with old boards. Anxious to test a theory, he found a rock on the floor of the shaft.

"Watch yourself," he warned before he pitched the rock up at the boards. It hit hard, jarring them, before dropping to the ground at his feet.

"They're not secured. Maybe we can knock them loose."

"What good will that do? We still can't climb out of the hole," Mariah said.

"Someone could hear us yelling. With the boards on, the sound is trapped."

"What about other ways out? Don't these shafts lead to tunnels?"

Baylor searched the earthen walls with the flashlight beam. "Sometimes, but most of these vertical shafts were air vents, or exploratory holes that go nowhere."

"If this one is an air vent, then the actual mine shaft would be below us?"

"Yeah." He glanced at her. Her face was coated in dirt, the sleeve of her blouse ripped almost off. He should have been paying attention topside, instead of kissing her. Maybe he'd have been able to protect her.

"What if we go down?"

He pulled in a breath. "We could try, but most of those old tunnels have caved in. We could go from thirty feet to the surface, to fifty feet from the surface."

"What are the odds someone will find us?"

A knot fisted in his gut. "Who knows we're out here?"

"My dad knows I'm on a stakeout, but he'd never figure I went for a horseback ride."

"My new ranch hand, Travis Priestly, doesn't show up until Monday. The horses will hightail it back to the barn…" Baylor paused. His summary of the situation was only making Mariah more tense and he had to keep her calm.

"Come on. I brought food and water. We'll eat and figure this out later."

She nodded, and he felt better. They sat down and he opened the saddlebag, taking out one of the sandwiches he'd made and cut in half. "We've got enough to last several days if we ration."

Mariah watched Baylor halve the half and took the sandwich from him. She wasn't really hungry, she decided as she bit into it, but if they were going to be trapped for any length of time down here, it was important to maintain their strength.

He pulled out the canteen and unscrewed the cap. "You first, one swallow."

She took the canteen from him, and took a drink, letting it moisten her parched throat. She handed it back to him. "Tell me we're going to get out of here."

"We're going to find a way out. I promise." She tried to smile, and took another bite of her sandwich, remembering the way he'd kissed her before their fateful plunge. She popped the last piece into her mouth, chewed and swallowed.

"Let's inventory what we have. Empty your pockets," he said, opening the saddlebag and digging inside.

Reaching into her pants, she pulled out everything she had. A package of gum, a handful of change, two paperclips, a mini-compact mirror, a couple of business cards and a used tissue. "That's it. A pitiful bunch of junk." She patted her pistol. "And this."

"I've got food, water, a pocketknife, flashlight, small first-aid kit, a horse tie-out line and a compass."

A zing of hope flashed through her as she stared at the coiled-up length of nylon rope. "How long?" She picked it up.

"Twenty feet."

Excitement streamed along her nerve endings and she stood up. "Maybe we could get it through the opening and tied off somehow."

Baylor stood up next to her and gauged the weight of the empty saddlebags. "We have to knock the boards out of the way. Let's add rocks."

Together, they filled the saddlebags with rocks and Baylor cinched the buckles tight. He uncoiled the rope and tied it securely around the wide leather strap that joined the two leather pouches together.

"Stand back." He tested the saddlebags, guessing they came in around fifteen pounds.

Stepping back as far as he could against the wall of the shaft, he tossed the loaded bags toward the opening.

Clunk. It hit the boards, dislodging one of them. A ray of sunlight streamed into the hole.

A dozen throws later, the boards their assailant had closed them in with had been knocked out of the way and light again shone through the jagged opening.

Baylor shoved his flashlight into his pocket, and folded onto the ground next to Mariah.

"Do you think you can climb out, if I put you on my shoulders?"

"I can try," she said, letting her head lull over and rest on his shoulder for an instant.

A rush of need washed through him as he put his arm around her, pulling her closer. "We'll get out of here," he said, stroking her hair even as he did the math. Their combined heights plus his arm length would still leave them ten feet short of the top.

He stared up at the opening. If he could get her close, maybe she could use the tree roots to climb out.

"Let's give it a try." He helped her to her feet. "I want you to use the roots once you stand up. Jerk on them first, make sure they'll hold you."

Mariah nodded.

Baylor bent over. "Climb on my shoulders." He braced himself, watching her pull off her shoes and shove them into the back waistband of her pants.

Caution wiggled along Mariah's spine and settled in her gut as she put her leg over Baylor's shoulders and sat down on his neck. He put his hands on her thighs and slowly raised her up.

She worked to keep her balance. Reaching out, she caught hold of a root and steadied herself. "Get as close to the wall as you can."

A spray of dirt rained down from the wall where she splayed her hand against it.

"Go easy," he warned. "The whole thing could come down."

Anxiety bit into her nerves. "Okay, I'm going to stand up." Balancing, using Baylor's raised hands, she put her left foot on his left shoulder.

"Come on, babe. You can do it," he coaxed as she wobbled, put the majority of her weight down on her left foot, and pushed up into a standing position, catching his other shoulder in the process.

"If you ever decide to quit chasing cows, we can join the circus."

He chuckled, and she felt the vibration through the bottoms of her stockinged feet. Reaching out, she took hold of a root, pulling at it like Baylor had told her to do. It held fast.

Stretching her other arm up, she gauged the distance to the opening. Eight feet, maybe ten. Searching, she locked her hand on another root, this one much larger. She felt it give when she jerked on it, and another shower of grit rained down on Baylor's head.

"So many of them are loose." She pulled on another one; it held. "If I can just find a couple that'll hold my weight."

She balanced, wobbled and regained her balance, feeling Baylor put his hands on her calves to steady her. "I think I can reach the top."

Feeling with her right foot, she found a toehold and put pressure on it. It held. Gingerly, she grasped the two tendrils she'd determined would hold, and stepped up off Baylor's shoulders.

Holding on for dear life, she felt the root give slightly, then hold fast. She caught her breath, and remained perfectly still, making sure it would continue to hold her before she searched for another foothold.

Focused on the opening, she climbed upward an inch at a time. Hope coursed in her veins and she could feel the sun's warmth on the top of her head.

She reached the top, grabbed a root and started to claw her way out of the hole.

Ping.

A bullet pierced the tendril above her thumb and fingers. The root snapped and decomposed in her hand.

She lost her balance, and launched backward, a scream ripped from her throat.

Chapter Four

Baylor braced for the impact, watching Mariah fall toward him in a hail of dirt and debris.

He caught her in his arms.

The earth dropped under his feet from the catch.

Before he could move they were falling again, to the floor of the shaft in a haze of dust and rock.

Fighting to hold on to her in the chaos, Baylor locked his arm around her waist.

They hit with a thud. The air rushed out of his lungs. He lay still until the dust cleared and opened his eyes in the darkness, still holding on to her.

"Are you okay?"

She shuddered. "Yeah. What happened?"

"The floor of the shaft gave way. We're in the tunnel below."

Baylor released her, sat up and pulled his flashlight out of his pocket. Dust polluted his lungs and he coughed, trying to clear them.

Turning on the light, he inched the beam along the

rock walls of the tunnel. It was narrow, maybe three feet wide. The debris from the collapsed air shaft blocked off the passageway in one direction.

Caution burned through him as he shined the light down the dark tunnel in the opposite direction. For the first time he considered the idea that this could be their final resting place.

"Come on, we've got to find the saddlebags if we can." Clamping the flashlight in his teeth, he started digging with his bare hands.

Mariah moved in next to him, digging, too.

"I found something." She pulled her compact up out of the dirt. "Just what every girl needs in the dark. A mirror. Damn."

She shoved it into her pocket, and went back to work digging. "This is better." She dragged up the saddlebags and dusted them off.

Baylor took the light out of his teeth. "Good job. We can live without the gum and my hat." He saw her smile in the scant lighting. She pulled her shoes out of her waistband and slipped them on.

"That way?" She pointed at the black hole to the north, as near as he could tell it was north.

"Yeah." Baylor stood up, slung the saddlebags over his shoulder and took her hand. He'd explored some of the tunnels as a teenager, but once his mom found out he'd been underground, she'd insisted the openings be sealed. Permanently.

He tamped down the worry that rocked through

him. They would find a way out, but for the time being they were safe down here from the shooter aboveground.

"Watch your step," he warned her as he shined the light on the uneven rock beneath their feet.

"Who made these tunnels?" Mariah asked, her grip tightening on his hand.

"Haven't you ever heard of the Montgomery Find Mine?"

"I didn't pay attention in Idaho history."

"Fifty years ago they hit a vein of gold down here a quarter of a mile wide, but it petered out five years later, and they abandoned the site."

Caution sluiced in Baylor's veins as they progressed along the tunnel, his flashlight beam shining on freshly drilled holes in the bedrock, ready to be plugged with dynamite and blasted. Sequential piles of ore lay ready to be transported out of the tunnel. Someone had been down here.

Recently.

He owned the mineral rights to the Bellwether, and as far as he knew, they were on Bellwether property.

The tunnel forked twenty feet ahead and they stopped.

"Which way?" Mariah asked, stepping forward.

"I'm not sure." He shined the light down the tunnel on the left, noting the downward slope of the rock floor. He did the same for the tunnel on the right, which looked level.

"Let's take the right tunnel, we don't want to go deeper underground."

"Sounds good." She latched on to his hand again, and he gave it a squeeze.

Baylor stepped into the tunnel, and paused. "Do you feel that?" A hint of air current pushed from out of the opening, moving the hair lying against his forehead. "It must open to the surface somewhere."

The beam coming from the flashlight dimmed. Baylor smacked it against his palm a couple of times and it glowed bright again. Relief spread through him. They'd be in real trouble without a light source.

Mariah dared to believe for the second time in the past hour. She didn't want to suffocate down here, and the brush of the breeze against her skin gave her hope.

"Thank God." The feel of Baylor next to her was the only thing that made the situation bearable. If she'd been down here alone, she'd have lost it by now.

Gingerly she followed him into the tunnel. Twenty feet, thirty feet, fifty feet. Ahead in the distance, she spotted a patch of light.

"Look at that!" Excitement surged in her veins and she fought the urge to race toward it, held back only by the feel of Baylor's hand holding hers, and a wave of tension in the air.

"Take it easy. There's a lot of dark between here and there."

Moving closer, she could see that the sliver of

light was no bigger than her arm, a slit in the earth. "It's too small to squeeze through."

Baylor shined the flashlight at the pile of rock below the crack. "I'm going to climb up and have a look, get an idea of where we are."

He handed her the flashlight and she aimed it so he could see. She watched him scramble up the mountain of loose rock, maybe six feet high, and peer out of the crack. "I can hear water. We must be close to the stream at the edge of the meadow."

He pulled back and shuffled down the mound toward her. The beam dimmed, and panic touched on her nerves as she shook the flashlight. "Dammit."

"Relax," Baylor coaxed, coming closer.

A scream gurgled in her throat as she stared at him in what was left of the light.

"Spiders!" With her hand she swiped at a couple of light brown-colored spiders crawling on the front of Baylor's shirt.

"Damn. Something's biting me on the back." He turned slightly, and the edge of light coming from the slit in the earth illuminated dozens of spiders crawling all over Baylor's shirt and over his shoulders.

"You're covered in them." Terror raked her body and she dropped the flashlight, slapping at the spiders.

She watched them drop to the floor and scatter in the dimming flashlight beam. One scrambled across her foot and she let out a scream that echoed against the ceiling of the tunnel.

Baylor pulled his shirt off and gave it a shake, freeing the nest of harmless brown spiders that he'd gotten into, but he had to calm Mariah. He could hear the panic in her voice.

"It's okay, I'm okay. They're harmless." He pulled his shirt back on and bent down, picking up the flashlight. It went out in his hand, but not before a flutter of wings whispered in the darkness.

"What was that!" Mariah shrieked.

He reached out and took hold of her.

Another set of wings beat the air, followed by a squeak and the drone of hundreds of bats coming alive inside the tunnel.

"Hold on." Baylor pulled Mariah closer, pressing her head against his chest as the swarm, awakened by their presence in the tunnel, reacted en masse.

Baylor tucked his head and waited for the onslaught to pass. High-pitched whistles and screeches echoed inside of the tunnel as the swarm of bats flocked past and moved through in the direction they'd come.

"Come on!" Taking Mariah's hand, he followed the sound.

She resisted, but he dragged her forward.

"They know the way." His reasoning seemed to penetrate her panic.

Back down the tunnel. Right into the one they hadn't chosen.

A rush of air greeted them the moment they

stepped into the corridor. He could feel the decline under his feet.

"Careful. Take it slow." Feeling along the wall of solid rock, he moved forward, still focused on the eerie cries of the bats ahead of them.

The tunnel turned slightly and Baylor slowed his pace. Squinting, he confirmed what he was seeing.

"There's light up ahead."

"I see it."

He moved quicker the closer he got, being able to make out the terrain under his feet in the light coming in through a large opening at the end of the tunnel.

The last bat darted out, and Baylor ducked and stepped through, still holding Mariah's hand.

He sucked in a breath of fresh air and looked around.

"I want to kiss the ground." Mariah sat down on the log that concealed the opening.

Caution warned Baylor they weren't safe yet. Not until they were back at the ranch. "Someone doesn't want this tunnel to be discovered. I'd guess it's whoever has been working in this mine and shooting at us."

"But I thought you said they closed it years ago."

"They did." Baylor stared into the woods, watching for any sign of movement. "Come on, we can't afford to stay here for long. He'll discover we're not in the tunnel anymore."

Mariah stood up. "Should we go for the horses?"

"Yeah. We're at the bottom of the meadow, just

into the timber. The horses should be that way." He pointed to the east, at the top of the trailhead.

Mariah came to her feet and pulled her gun out of its holster.

The woods hummed with the buzz of insects. Somewhere a woodpecker hammered his beak against a tree, boring out a hole.

She scanned the forest as she hurried along the trail behind Baylor, fighting the sensation of being watched. God only knew how many places their tormenter could hide. He could take another shot at them and they'd never see it coming.

Baylor picked up the pace and she broke into a jog behind him. They rounded the last corner and came to a stop.

The horses were gone.

A chill rocked her body as she turned around, pointing her pistol into the woods as she scanned behind them.

They needed to find the horses and get off the mountain.

"Jericho and Texas will head for the ranch. They're probably standing in the road wondering where we are."

Baylor studied the scattering of hoof prints and shoe prints in the loose soil where the horses had been tied.

"Do you suppose they got spooked and broke loose when the gunshots went off?" Mariah asked.

"Doubt it. They're both used to rifle fire. They'd

have stayed put." There. There it was on the opposite side of the tree. "I found something."

They moved around to where he could get a clear look at the single boot track in the dirt. "They were untied. Probably by whoever did the shooting. He managed to wipe away the rest of his prints, all except for this one."

Mariah stared at the print, memorizing its shape and trying to gauge its size. She could see the drag marks where something had been rubbed over the ground, erasing the rest of the prints. "He didn't want us to know he'd been here."

"That, or be identified. Let's get out of here." Baylor started for the trail.

The sun beat down on them as they worked their way down the steep decline that switched back and forth across the mountain. They stopped a couple of times for a drink from the canteen Baylor carried in the saddlebag, but always he stayed vigilant, watching, anticipating another shooting spree.

An hour later they descended the last fifty feet of trail and stepped out onto the main road.

Harley Neville stood next to his truck holding the reins of the horses. "Dammit, Baylor, don't scare me like that. My old ticker can't take it. I came around the corner and here they were. What the hell happened to you?"

Baylor smiled at his neighbor and walked over to him, checking the horses over to make sure they were okay. He rubbed Jericho's neck, noting the broken rein. He'd probably stepped on it in his hurry to get down off the mountain.

"We had some trouble with an abandoned mine shaft, but we're okay. Thanks for holding my horses." He took both sets of reins. "You see anyone else come down out of here?"

"Not in the past hour. But I did pass Ray Buckner on his four-wheeler about half an hour ago. He was in a mighty big hurry."

Baylor knew the man, had met him a time or two since he'd been working on the Turner ranch as a hand.

"He didn't by any chance have a rifle with him, did he?"

"Don't know, but he had a long gun scabbard strapped on the front handlebars."

A surge of caution flared just under Baylor's skin. Was it possible Ray had taken those shots at them? Boarded them up in the shaft?

"Thanks, Harley."

"You bet." Harley climbed into his pickup and headed east toward his cabin.

"Are you up for the ride home?"

"Yeah. But I plan to talk to Ray Buckner, find out what he was doing out here."

Baylor handed Mariah the reins to her horse and tied the saddlebag on. "Things got carried away up in the meadow. If I overstepped a boundary, I'm sorry." He shot her a glance and saw her cheeks turn pink.

"I'm not." She mounted up, sitting tall in the saddle as a slight smile pulled at her lips. Lips he could still feel against his own. Hell, if they hadn't been interrupted, who knew where that kiss might have led?

He mounted up and turned his horse for home as Mariah rode next to him in silence. Tension knotted the muscles between his shoulder blades and he contemplated how hard it would be to stop if he got close to her again. He couldn't let it happen. Couldn't risk his heart. Not again, not on a lady cop who didn't trust him.

MARIAH LAID THE once-white washcloth on the bathroom counter and stared at her reflection in the mirror. She'd managed to scrub all of the mine shaft dirt off her face and she felt almost human again. Baylor had loaned her one of his T-shirts in place of her torn blouse.

She glanced at her watch—three o'clock, plenty of time to question Ray Buckner before she headed for the station.

Baylor stood in the middle of the living room waiting for her.

A low whistle came from between his pursed lips. "You clean up good, Detective."

"Thanks, and I see you found another hat."

He tipped it and smiled. "What's a cowboy without his hat?"

The gesture set her thoughts in motion and she

knew she was in trouble. There was nothing about him that wasn't attractive to her.

"We better take the pickup. The road into the Turner place is rough. We might need four-wheel drive." He pulled the keys out of his pocket and moved to the front door, opening it for her.

She walked outside and he followed. "I plan to press criminal charges, if we can get the evidence on Ray Buckner."

"I never would have figured him for something like this." Baylor opened the passenger's-side door for her. She brushed past him and got into the truck, her skin on fire where they'd made contact.

"Sometimes the worst of the worst are right under your nose. You pass them every day, and you don't know it."

He closed the door, went around to the driver's side and climbed in. "How do you live with that, Mariah? Do you look at everyone with suspicion?"

She sobered, considering his philosophical question. She'd been wondering the same thing as of late, and she could track her new contemplations right back to him.

"Yeah. I guess I do. I have to, or I wouldn't be able to do my job. The bad guys would take over the streets."

He fired up the engine. "I like to see the best in everyone."

"You mean, hope for the best in everyone?"

His jaw tightened, as he put the truck in Reverse.

"No. See. Hope just means you have expectations that may never be realized. Seeing the best is physical. The old adage, actions speak louder than words, applies more times than not."

She sat in silence, absorbing the gist of his words. In her world, those gut reactions, those little warning voices in her head, they were all just speculation. Sometimes they were right, sometimes they were wrong. That's what led her to him. In his world, physical actions really did determine a person's character. Like his saving her from freezing to death. She swallowed, staring out the window as they drove down the driveway and out onto the main road. Her line of work really had changed her view of humankind.

"Where's the Turner ranch?"

"Just before the first bridge over the Salmon, we'll take a right. They run mostly sheep, but they've got some cattle."

"Maybe I should deputize you, in case there's trouble." She glanced at him and watched a not-on-your-life smirk spread on his lips.

"I didn't think so, but I had to try."

"I know you did." Baylor tightened his grip on the steering wheel and stared straight ahead. Every nerve in his body was attuned to her, but mentally he pushed back. Caring for the beautiful detective was off-limits.

"I know the Turners. Do you want me to approach them?"

"Sure. That might help us get our hands on Buckner."

"They're good people, Mariah. They'll cooperate."

She nodded. "Okay."

Baylor turned right and followed the narrow road back into the Turner ranch. Twenty minutes later, he pulled up in front of the house, a single-level ranch style surrounded by a covered porch.

The Turners and the McCulloughs had been friends for years. The Turners had been some of the first folks to offer help after Amy drowned. They'd treated him more like a son than a friend. In fact, they'd been some of the only people who believed in him while James Endicott had tried his best to prosecute him for Amy's death.

Maude Turner was the first one out of the door, and she stepped out onto the porch wearing an apron. Her husband, Clive, was right behind her.

Baylor climbed out of the pickup and headed for the porch. "Maude, Clive. I'd like you to meet Detective Mariah Ellis."

"Detective?" Maude repeated, the welcoming smile slipping from her face.

"I'm with the county sheriff's department," Mariah said, stepping forward. "We had some trouble this morning. I'd like to speak with one of your ranch hands."

"What sort of trouble?" Clive asked.

"Someone took rifle shots at us up in the meadow on the east side of the Bellwether. A witness saw your ranch hand, Ray Buckner, out there on a four-wheeler."

"He was up there all right. Tracking a pack of wolves that have been killing our sheep for over a month. But I can tell you he wasn't armed with a rifle, just a .22 sidearm to protect himself if he needed to."

"Where can we find him, Mr. Turner?" Mariah asked.

"Montana. He left two hours ago. He's at a rodeo in Missoula this week. He won't be back until Friday."

Mariah felt the wind go out of her sails. "Do you mind if we have a look at the four-wheeler?"

"Go ahead. It's down by the bunkhouse." Clive pointed toward the spot where a huge barn stood. Next to it was a long row of individual cabins.

"Thank you, Mr. Turner." Mariah pulled a card out of her back pocket and handed it to Clive. "Have him call when he gets back. I'd like to know if he saw anything up there this morning."

Clive took the card, looked at it and put it in his shirt pocket. "Can I interest you two in a bite of supper?"

"No, thanks." Mariah said. "I've got to get back to town."

"I'll take a rain check." Baylor tipped his hat and followed Mariah back to the truck. They climbed in and waved at the Turners.

"You were right. They're nice people." She stared

out the window as Baylor fired up the pickup and drove down to the bunkhouse. "How long have you known them?"

"Since I was a kid. They bought the ranch when I was in the fifth grade."

"They knew Amy then?"

"Yeah. When we first got married, Maude tried to teach her how to survive up here. I don't know that Maude ever gave up on Amy, even after she made it clear she didn't want to be here."

Mariah's heart squeezed in her chest, and she glanced at Baylor. His jaw was locked; he stared straight ahead, his shoulders rigid.

"I'm sorry. It's really none of my business." She regretted the inquiry, wishing she could take it back.

"It was no secret she hated my way of life, and she didn't mind telling anyone who'd listen. Maude did the best she could to help Amy adjust. After she drowned, Clive and Maude were the only ones who didn't look at me like I was some sort of a killer." Baylor pulled up in front of the bunk- house where the four-wheeler was parked, and turned off the engine.

"Endicott did his best to convict me. He ques- tioned everyone on the river including the Turners, and then some. I couldn't walk down the street in town without hearing the whispers."

Mariah sobered. For the first time she realized how devastating Amy's death must have been for him, and the aftermath could well have driven him over the edge. But enough to hurt James Endicott?

"In this country you're innocent until proven guilty. I'm sorry you had to endure his zealous attack."

"I survived." He pushed his hat back and looked at her. "But I've always wondered why he had it in for me." Baylor opened the door and climbed out of the truck.

Mariah pondered the unanswered question as she got out of the pickup and circled the four-wheeler. She flipped open the hardcover rifle scabbard mounted in front of the handlebars.

Lying in the foam-insulated holder was a rifle.

Caution laced through her. She had enough probable cause to seize the gun, but she didn't have a slug to compare it to in a test fire. Those bullets were all up in the meadow, buried in the dirt around the mine shaft.

"So much for him only packing a .22."

Baylor let out a low whistle. "Damn. I would never have believed it."

"We'll have to go back to the meadow with a metal detector, and a CSI to recover one of the slugs from the ground so they can do a ballistics comparison."

"Why would he shoot at us?" Baylor couldn't still the doubt looping in his mind. Killing someone was serious business.

What did Ray Buckner possibly have to gain?

Chapter Five

CSI Ryan Worchester stood up holding a mini-shovel in one hand and a bullet in the other.

Mariah dropped her sunglasses down on her nose and stared at it. "What do you think?"

"I won't know until I get it into the lab, but it's a rifle slug. Too big to have come from a pistol."

She pushed her glasses back into place and glanced over to where Baylor stood, his hat pushed low on his head, arms crossed as he surveyed the meadow.

"Does the chief know about this?" Ryan asked, dropping the shovel and fishing for an evidence bag in the pocket of his pants.

"I didn't mention that someone was shooting at us, in so many words, but I've got a lead I'm following up. Just do the ballistics comparison with the rifle I brought in yesterday evening."

"Okay. I should have the results in a couple of days." Ryan dropped the bullet into a baggie, zipped it closed and put it in his pocket. "Damn beautiful spot to be shot at." He looked around the meadow.

"Yeah. But I'd rather enjoy the scenery than have to take cover behind it. Be careful getting out of here, and stay on the path." She glanced over at the vertical shaft that had almost been their grave.

She followed Ryan back to where Baylor held their rides down off the mountain.

"You found a bullet?" he asked.

"Yes, we've got what we need to compare it with the rifle we found on the four-wheeler Buckner was riding."

Baylor nodded, glad to wrap things up in the meadow. For the first time in his life, the setting seemed hostile to him. The feeling of being watched had invaded his senses more than once since they'd first entered the area this morning, and he couldn't shake it.

"You take the lead, Mariah." He handed her the reins to Jericho. "Do you need help, Ryan?"

CSI Worchester had ridden Whiskey to the meadow, an old mare Baylor had retired but still had an affection for. She was kid-gentle, perfect for an inexperienced rider.

"No. I think I've got this." Ryan put his foot into the stirrup and mounted up, grabbing a hold of the saddle horn.

Baylor handed him the reins, and mounted Texas. "I'll take up the rear."

The trio moved along the trail down out of the

meadow, and Baylor didn't breathe easy until they were riding up the driveway to the ranch. He had some investigating of his own to do, but it would have to wait.

The crunch of gravel under tires brought his head around and he moved over to the side of the drive, as Travis Priestly slowed and pulled up next to him.

"Hey." Travis leaned out of the open window of his vehicle.

"Go ahead and come up to the house. I'll show you where you're going to bunk." He liked Travis. He was trying his hand at ranching for the first time through a work study program out of a college in Montana, and Baylor had jumped on the chance to tutor the kid.

Travis rolled past him, braked in the driveway and climbed out of his car.

Baylor reined in Texas, climbed down and tied him next to the other horses. CSI Worchester was already walking toward his vehicle, and gave a wave.

"You've got company," Mariah said as she came toward him.

"He's my ranch hand for the summer. Come on, I'd like you to meet him. He's a nice kid."

They walked over to where Travis was rummaging in the trunk of his car.

"Travis, I'd like you to meet Mariah Ellis. She's a detective from the sheriff's department."

"How do you do?" Travis shook her hand. "I didn't know they made cops like you."

Mariah pulled in a breath and smiled at him. He was a good-looking kid, with a close-cropped haircut, brown eyes, brown hair and a nice grin. She liked him. "Well, thanks."

She turned back to Baylor. "I've got to get back to the station."

"I'll walk you to your car."

He moved along next to her and she caught wind of his woodsy scent.

"I'll let you know what Ryan finds out, ASAP. If that bullet belongs to Buckner's rifle, we'll arrest him immediately." She stopped next to her car, and turned to stare up into his face. "Watch yourself."

He smiled. "You do the same."

"I will."

MARIAH LEANED BACK in her desk chair and stared out the window at the boring parking lot.

An unsettled feeling had dogged her since she'd climbed in her car at the Bellwether Ranch yesterday morning and waved goodbye to Baylor.

She felt like an idiot for kissing him back in the meadow, and she'd compromised her investigation to a point of no return. She'd lost what little objectivity she had left and she planned to tell her father, if she could get up the nerve. He was an intuitive man. He'd begin a line of questioning that would box her in and the truth would be the only way out.

The slap of his office door against the kick stop brought her head around.

"Ellis, get in here!" he ordered in the gruff tone of voice he saved for those times when he was agitated, but she knew it was just flash.

Mariah sighed as she stood up and strode toward the office. She doubted he knew about the kiss, so what had fired him up?

"Come in and close the door."

She did as she was told and plopped down in the stiff brown chair in front of his desk, feeling like an unruly kid about to be grounded for a month.

"These showed up in the mail this afternoon." He tossed a packet of bagged evidence photos down in front of her.

Mariah leaned forward and picked them up. Her breath caught up in her throat as she studied the images, flipping through them one by one.

"Can you identify them?" he asked.

"Yeah. It's James Endicott and…Amy McCullough."

A measure of disbelief rubbed holes in her thinking. How was it possible? How could it be? The images had been shot at night and showed a half-naked Amy locked in a compromising clinch with Endicott. Mariah flipped through the pictures one more time, noting that each was more intimate than the last.

Letting out the breath she'd been holding, she

tossed them back onto her dad's desk, feeling a weight descend on her. "Any prints? Any idea who sent them?"

"No on both counts. But they're at least a year old. Amy McCullough died a year ago today."

Mariah sobered. Her throat tightened. A wave of emotion plowed her over. The pain Baylor must be experiencing today, and now these.

"Endicott and Amy were having an affair." The words were like acid coming up in her throat.

Ted Ellis thumped his desk. "This could be a motive for Baylor McCullough. If he knew his wife was sleeping with Endicott, he could have snapped. Maybe Endicott was justified in going after him for Amy's death. Maybe he really did have something to do with it."

Mariah's heart squeezed in her chest and she tried to get her cop brain around it. She didn't want to believe it, but there it was in full color. Most crimes of passion involved infidelity, jealousy, rage. Was Baylor capable of murder over his wife's affair?

"I've got a uniformed officer en route to pick him up for questioning. He'll be in your interrogation room within the hour. Press him hard, Mariah, make him account for his whereabouts the day Endicott went missing."

Things were spinning out of control, she realized as she stood up. Was it possible? Her mind wanted to believe the incriminating evidence in the photos would be enough to push any loving husband over the edge, but her heart couldn't.

BAYLOR STARED AT THE gray walls of the interrogation room, a bland cubicle that reeked of trouble. Unfortunately he'd had the experience of seeing it once before. A year to the day he'd lost Amy, but he'd survived the aftermath. The fact that he'd even been suspected of not trying to save her from drowning sent a charge of irritation rattling through him.

The door to the room opened and Mariah Ellis stepped inside.

He sucked in a breath to ease the tension knotting his shoulders. He could see it on her face, see it in the narrowing of her eyes as she studied him.

Contemplation.

She pulled out the chair across the table from him and sat down before laying a manila folder out in front of her and opening it.

"These showed up here this afternoon. Did you know about this?" There was an accusatory tone in her voice. He bristled, glancing down at the five pictures she laid out in front of him.

Anger and pain churned his emotions as he stared down at the photos. He reached out and picked up the most incriminating of the group. A shot taken through a slit in a curtained window. Amy and Endicott locked in a kiss, minus their clothes.

"How did I miss this?" He swallowed. "How in

the hell did I miss this? No wonder he came after me when she died. He wanted someone to pay for taking her from him."

Mariah's heart squeezed in her chest and her throat tightened around her words. She hadn't intended to torture him with the pictures, but that's exactly what she was doing.

"I'm sorry you had to discover the truth like this."

He rocked back in his chair, his lips formed in a grim line. "I knew there was someone else, but Endicott?" He shook his head slowly. "Why?"

She didn't have the answer, probably never would, but she suddenly disliked Amy McCullough. What had pushed her to infidelity when her own husband was so…gorgeous? She stiffened, wishing the wayward path of thought to meander somewhere else. Physically sizing up Baylor wasn't part of her job, getting a firm verifiable alibi was.

"Where were you on April the fifth after 4:30 p.m.?"

His eyes narrowed. "I get it, you think these pictures prove something?"

"A possible…." she cleared her throat "…motive."

"We're done here, Detective. I want my lawyer."

His words slammed into her like a physical blow. She'd had suspects lawyer up time and again, so why did it upset her that Baylor McCullough was doing the same thing?

"Please, Baylor. You have to tell me where you were and what you were doing on the fifth."

He sat back and crossed his arms over his broad chest.

Time stretched as she waited, waited for an answer that would alleviate the creeping edge of concern that wrapped around her heart. "I can verify it. You'll be cleared."

His features didn't soften.

Why was she pleading with him? She'd never pleaded with a suspect in her life, but he was different.

She pushed back her chair and stood up, gathering the scandalous photos, watching his eyes follow their progression as she put them back into the folder.

"I'm sorry." Her breath caught in her throat; her brain flooded with sympathy. The emotions were wrong. The situation suffocating.

She moved toward the door. "You're free to use the phone to contact your lawyer."

"Mariah. Wait."

She froze in midstep and turned around, hope generating in her mind and body as she stared at him.

He stood up. "I'd like to help you, but no one saw me on the fifth. I was riding herd in the high country. I saddled up before dawn and returned just after dark. I didn't speak to a soul who can verify it, and my cow dog Bess isn't talking."

A brief smile pulled at her mouth, but the seriousness of the situation pushed it down. "That's all I needed to know. You're free to go."

"I'll never be free to go." He stepped past her and she felt a charge build between them. The memory of his lips on hers as they lay in the grass was so vivid it tested her resolve, but somewhere in her mind she believed him. Baylor McCullough was an honorable man.

"Will you take a polygraph?"

"No." He reached for the doorknob and she fought the urge to touch him. They'd already experienced intimacy, and she found herself drawn to him, but she resisted her primal urge.

"Derrick Hastings is good."

He stared down at her, so close she could see the muscle along his jawline jump.

"This is about Amy, isn't it?" He leaned closer.

Her heart rate shot up. "No."

His scent invaded her senses, a mix of outdoor air and the forest. Her desire hit overdrive.

"What she did with Endicott was wrong. She was your wife. I don't understand how she could do it when she had someone like…" The last word died on her tongue as she stared up at him. His eyelids closed slightly, his blue-gray eyes taking her in with a sultry gaze that could have dissolved granite.

Mariah felt her knees go weak, overtaken by the seductive line of his body as he relaxed and leaned against the doorjamb.

"Is that a hint of belief coming from you? A maybe-he's-telling-the-truth admission?"

Heat burned inside her and blazed onto her cheeks. "Murderers don't usually go around saving lives. It's not an admission, just an observation."

He smiled slow and easy, raising her level of desire to white-hot, just before the door opened and she nearly fell into the arms of the chief of police.

"Detective Ellis. I need a word."

BAYLOR STEPPED OUT of the interrogation room into the hallway, but not before the sound of Chief Ellis's raised voice hit his eardrums.

He lifted his gaze to the exit sign at the end of the corridor and tried to stay focused as he put one foot in front of the other, listening to the sound of his own boots hitting the polished tiles. Every nerve in his body was ready to explode.

Pushing through the double glass doors, he walked out onto the massive cement steps of the station. Hell, he didn't even have a ride home, but somehow that didn't matter. The world as he'd known it had just imploded with Amy at the center.

Striding down the steps, he turned left on Main Street and started walking. Had she needed more attention? He'd always known the ranching life didn't suit her. Too much solitude for someone as fun-loving as she'd been and not enough action to make her happy.

A knot fisted in his gut as he mentally recalled the details of the pictures that Mariah had laid out on the table in front of him.

Mariah. He had to believe the information had torn her apart as well. He'd caught a glimmer of pain in her eyes. That gut-level reaction when you discover you've misread someone's moral compass.

The toot of a car horn drew his attention, and he watched her pull her white sedan in next to the curb and roll down her window.

"Need a ride?"

He stopped walking and stared at her, watching the way the breeze moved her hair around her face. It was a face he liked.

"It's department policy."

"In that case." He moved around to the passenger's side and climbed in next to her.

"I wouldn't want to mess with policy." He gave her a sideways glance and watched her smile again, something that eased the tension in his body to a level he could tolerate. He was pretty sure she'd gotten an earful after he'd dodged a bullet and left the interrogation room.

"I've got to make a quick stop by the house, and we can get on the road."

"No problem." He put on his seat belt and leaned back. "I take it your boss isn't too happy?"

She looked both ways and pulled out onto Main. "Let's just say Endicott's missing persons case is stalled. My father is one step away from calling the FBI. If we can't catch a break, and soon, we'll have the feds crawling all over the place."

He hated the sound of that. They wouldn't go easy on him. They'd make his life hell, and maybe hers, too. "I'll take the damn poly, if it'll help."

She braked at the stoplight and turned left onto Sycamore. "I can get the examiner out of Spokane down here next week."

He watched a smile turn her mouth as she maneuvered the car onto Cottonwood Street and pull into the driveway of her house.

"Give me a time and place. I'll be there."

She put the car in Park and shut off the engine. "It's as much for you as it is for me."

"Somehow I doubt that." He saw her wince. "I know I haven't done anything wrong. You're the only one who needs convincing."

Mariah didn't dare look at him for fear he'd see right through her. More than anything she wanted to believe him on all counts. "I'll just be a minute."

She pulled open the door latch and climbed out of the car, with her emotions at war. A battle of good cop, bad cop ragged inside of her. She'd settle for just cop at this point, because she wasn't acting much like one where Baylor McCullough was concerned.

Fiddling with her key, she shoved it into the lock and turned the knob.

She pushed open the door and the pungent odor of turpentine hit her full force.

Mariah backed out onto the porch nearly colliding with Baylor, who'd gotten out of the car and now stood next to her.

"What is it? What's wrong?"

"Someone broke into my house!"

Baylor took a step toward the entry and stared into the once-inviting living room.

Anger stirred in his blood as he looked at the beautiful painting he'd admired the first time he'd been in her home. Someone had doused it with turpentine. The once-majestic images now streaked and running down the canvas, dissolved by the paint thinner. He didn't paint, but he was pretty sure an artist and her art were like a cowboy and his favorite horse—inseparable.

He put his arm around her shoulders, caution coursing through him. What if she'd been home alone when the intruder broke in?

"I've got to call this in. Maybe the jerk left something behind." Her voice broke. "Something I can nail him with." She moved away from him and he followed, determined to protect her somehow from the ugliness inside. The destruction of her artwork, the seed of her passion, the key to her soul, he guessed.

He listened to her phone call and waited with her until the first cruiser rolled up on scene before stepping back into the shadows.

Was the sniper attempt on their lives somehow related to this? And if so, how in the hell did he look after a cop whose job it was to serve and protect?

SHE HAD TO QUESTION Ray Buckner, Mariah decided as the last of the crime scene investigators put their equipment away and stepped out of her living room. He was supposed to be back from Missoula today.

CSI Worchester and his team's hours of searching hadn't revealed a single fingerprint or one identifiable speck of evidence with which to nail the SOB who'd invaded her home. He'd come through a rear window to trash the place, and left her feeling vulnerable in a setting she'd always felt safe in before.

Baylor stood in the doorway between the kitchen and dining room, arms crossed as he studied her. "They'll catch him, Mariah."

She wished she could take hold of his words and believe them, but she'd seen her share of unsolved break-ins.

"With prints, you're right, but he didn't leave anything. And then there's this." She motioned to the destroyed painting on the wall behind her couch. "Why would he do that? There's a personal message there. Deface my art, you deface me." A shudder vibrated through her, leaving her exhausted and confused.

"How well do you know Ray Buckner?"

"I've met him a couple of times in my travels, seemed like a nice enough guy."

"How old?"

"Early twenties. You think he had something to do with this?" Baylor pulled out a chair at the dining-room table across from her and sat down.

"I don't know. He could be warning me to back off my investigation. I just need to talk to him."

"I know he's a saddle bronc rider. The Turners said he was rodeoing. He'll probably be back at the Salmon River Rodeo this weekend."

She hadn't thought of that angle. The annual Salmon River Rodeo was coming up. Two days of saddle bronc and bareback riding, barrel racing, bull bucking, team roping and wild cow milking fun that left the town packed to the rafters with cowboys, their horses and plenty of fans.

"Would you mind pointing him out for me?"

"Love to." Baylor smiled and her anxiety melted into her shoes, the ones she planned to exchange for a pair of cowboy boots come rodeo time tomorrow.

Chapter Six

Mariah moved through the crowd of fans clogging the narrow street next to the rodeo grounds. Stadium lights situated around the area hummed and illuminated the dust in the night air being kicked up by the rodeo events transpiring in the fenced arena.

The early evening air was crisp, and she buttoned her denim jacket, the one she'd donned along with a gray Stetson to take the coppy-looking edge off.

After running Ray Buckner's name through her computer, she'd discovered he had several outstanding warrants. Her gut feeling was that he'd run. Assuming she wanted to take him in on the warrants.

Glancing into the crowd, she spotted Baylor moving at a slow pace some thirty feet from her. His height put him at an advantage, along with a cowboy hat pulled low on his head.

A zing of desire pulsed inside of her. He was a walking distraction, and she searched for another focus, finding it in the tangy smell of barbecued ribs and onion rings that wafted from the food vendors operating along the street on the opposite side of the arena and grandstands.

Trying to look casual, she stopped and flipped open her program, searching the list of events until she found Ray Buckner's name in the third section of saddle bronc riders. He'd drawn a horse called Sonny, and he'd be riding it if she wasn't hauling him into the station.

Mariah closed the program and searched out Baylor again, spotting him near the main gate, his elbow resting on the top rail of the fence as he scanned the crowd.

He made eye contact with her, pulled his hat off and put it back on. The signal that he'd spotted Ray somewhere in the wave of people pushing to get into the rodeo.

Mariah's heart rate kicked up a beat. She remained focused on Baylor as she started toward him.

He gave three quick nods.

She followed his line of sight, spotting Ray Buckner as he headed for the gate leading back in behind the bucking chutes and catch pens with a bronc saddle slung over his shoulder, wearing a bright orange and white striped shirt.

She was on him in ten quick strides.

"Ray Buckner, Detective Ellis, county sheriff's department. I need to talk to you."

Before she could flash her badge, he bolted into the crowd of cowboys streaming through the narrow gate.

Adrenaline surged through Mariah's veins.

She took off after him, badge in hand as she bumped and pushed her way in behind the bucking chutes.

Getting her bearings, she saw the bobbing motion of his black hat, and raced after him, spotting him for a brief moment when he turned to see if he'd lost her.

"Ray! Ray!" Mariah waved, shouting above the drone of excited voices, but he kept moving away from her, deeper and deeper into the area where the gleaming lights surrounding the arena didn't penetrate.

She rushed to the end of the bucking chutes and stopped, trying to ascertain where he'd gone. She spotted him rushing down a narrow corridor, and gave chase.

There were fewer cowboys the farther into the back of the rodeo grounds she pushed.

She could hear the rustle of restless livestock in the maze of pens. Caution zipped through her for an instant when a bull bellowed in the holding pen beside her.

She tried to get her bearings in the dark, cramped and dusty corridor.

Where was Buckner?

She felt a push from behind at the precise moment the small gate she was standing next to opened, and she was shoved through it into the holding pen.

Mariah hit the ground on her belly and raised her head to stare in horror at dozens of hooves.

Reality dawned hard and fast as she rolled to the left, a hoof barely missing her head.

The massive animal came at her again head down, horns poised to gore her if given the chance.

She went on autopilot. Move, keep moving.

Where was the gate? She'd have to stand to open it.

She could shoot the bull, but there were a dozen more just like him in the pen.

Mariah glanced up at the fence. The rungs were six inches apart. Too narrow for her to slip through. She'd have to use the gate. If she timed it right, she could stand up and make it through before he killed her, and she had no doubt that the eighteen-hundred-pound Brahma bull snorting and pawing the earth a few feet away could do just that in a matter of seconds.

"Mariah! Up here. I'll pull you out."

The sound of Baylor's voice was a relief, and she scrambled to her feet just as the bull lunged, slamming into her body with his head and hooking her with his horn.

A sting of pain shot through her left arm and she saw stars for an instant, trying to suck in a breath.

She was lifted up off her feet by the force of the blow.

Baylor bolted up the fence, lodged his feet in one of the rungs, bent over at the waist and snagged Mariah from the bull. He then raised her up above the enormous animal before he could finish her off.

He set her on the other side and jumped down, pulling her into his arms.

His heartbeat hammered in his eardrums, drowning out the cheers of fans as an animal tossed its rider before the eight-second buzzer.

He felt her sag in his arms and looked down at her. Blood stained the front of his shirt and the sleeve of her jacket gapped open.

"Mariah?" Fear constricted his chest, making it hard to breathe. Time ground to a stop, images clicking by in slow motion. He was there again. In the water, a prisoner of that night a year ago. Amy...he had to save Amy. The car filled with water. Icy water. Terror's crushing power dug into his brain and immobilized him.

"He hooked me. I need the EMTs."

The whisper of Mariah's words cut through the replayed trauma stuck in his brain and sucked him back into the present.

"Where?"

"My arm."

He scooped her up and laced through the crowd heading for the ambulance and the EMTs who could do for her what no one had been able to do for Amy, not even him.

Save her.

She was fragile and small in his arms. Urgency bubbled up in him and he quickened his step, not satisfied until he reached the EMS staff.

"A bull hooked her," he said as he sat her down on the back step of the ambulance.

Already he missed the feel of her in his arms, and he watched as they took a pair of scissors to the tattered sleeve of her jacket and exposed her arm.

A gash marred her skin just above her elbow. The bleeding had almost stopped, but she was going to need stitches.

"You're lucky he didn't catch the brachial artery," the EMT said as he cleaned the gash and applied a sterile dressing. "You need to roll up to the hospital and have it stitched."

Mariah nodded and felt suddenly nauseous. She'd been inches from death. If it hadn't been for Baylor…

"Would cowboy Ray Buckner please come to the registration window to sign your release? They're holding your bronc." The announcer's voice rasping over the loudspeaker caught her attention.

Concern jetted through her. If Ray hadn't signed his release so he could ride, that could only mean he'd taken off after she'd tried to question him. Was he the one who'd shoved her into the holding pen with the bulls?

"Can we get a couple of EMTs down here behind the bucking chutes?" The announcer's voice held an edge of panic in it and Mariah stood up.

Baylor was next to her before she could take a step. "Relax, sweetheart. He hit you hard."

She touched his hand and felt a jolt of attraction arch between them. "Yeah, but something's up. Ray

Buckner didn't sign his release. He probably took off after I chased him."

"You'll find him, Mariah. You know where he lives."

It was true. There wasn't much chance he'd slip completely away. She planned to call in uniformed backup before she got to the hospital. They'd find Ray Buckner.

She watched two EMTs grab their jump kit and disappear into the crowd behind the bucking chutes.

"I need to take your blood pressure," another EMT said.

The cuff tightened on her arm and slowly released. She jotted down the results on a run sheet. "You be sure to get your arm stitched up within six hours."

"I will," Mariah promised, as the EMT took the BP cuff off her arm.

The announcer's voice come over the PA system in a panicky tone. "Can we please have the arena cleared immediately? We're going to release the bulls from the holding pen. Please clear the arena."

Mariah stood up, feeling tension stiffen the air over the entire area. Baylor must have felt it, too, because he stepped closer to her.

"We need an officer down behind the bucking chute."

Mariah felt for her gun with her right hand, content when she locked her hand around the butt of it. "I'm going."

Baylor was two steps behind her as a loud groan went up from the crowd. Dodging through people, she made it to the now-empty holding pen where she'd nearly been killed only moments before.

A grim-faced cowboy opened the gate for her when she flashed her badge.

Inside, the EMTs worked at a numbing pace doing CPR on a cowboy, trying to save his life.

Mariah swallowed hard as she stepped closer, catching a glimpse of a familiar-looking shirtsleeve. Orange and white. Horror rushed through her bloodstream, just as Baylor put his arm around her shoulders, stabilizing her on her wobbly knees.

A battered, bloody, half-dead Ray Buckner lay in the muck of the bull pen where he'd been stomped and gored.

Uniformed officers attempted to shield the scene from the crowd that had gone silent.

She turned into Baylor, burying her face against his chest to shut out the horror of the trauma unfolding in the dirt.

Had she caused this? In Ray's panic to escape, had he fallen in the bull pen? Or had he been pushed in just like her?

She pulled herself together and looked up at Baylor. His mouth was set in a hard line, which softened as he stared down at her.

"That could have been you."

Mariah swallowed. "But it's not."

He nodded, and the grim set of his jawline relaxed. "Do you think he was pushed?"

"Yeah. Considering the same thing happened to me. This pen is a crime scene. And the bastard who did it is out there, somewhere." She took in the sheer number of people and sighed. The odds she'd find him were slim to none, and she hadn't even had a chance to get a look at her assailant in the darkness behind the chute.

"I'll speak to the uniforms, give a statement and head for the hospital."

Baylor nodded, released her and moved toward the gate.

She headed for Officers Duffy and Bradshaw, who worked crowd control.

Scanning the faces of the curious onlookers, she searched for anything or anyone who didn't jive, but there was no one who stood out. No one wearing an "I did it" sign posted above their Stetson, and she could only pray that Ray Buckner lived to tell her how he'd found his way into the bull pen.

"What the hell happened to you?" Officer Bob Duffy said as he looked at her arm.

"I got too close to a bull, just like Ray Buckner." She motioned to where the EMTs still worked on him. "I don't think this was an accident. You need to call it in, have CSI Worchester and his team come down to have a look. One of you needs to ride to the hospital with Buckner, in case he says anything."

Bob Duffy shook his head. "You're kidding, right? There's no way any evidence could survive this mess."

Mariah looked around at the bull pen, which was a virtual quagmire. Bob was probably right. "Do it anyway. You never know."

He nodded and turned away, pulling his handheld radio off his belt to make the call.

"I'll ride in with him," Officer Bradshaw said before turning and making his way over to where EMS worked.

Mariah searched for Baylor and saw him waiting for her next to the gate.

Working her way toward him, she couldn't shake the feeling that the assailant was standing in the crowd, watching, and that fact bothered her.

BAYLOR WATCHED THE doctor put the last stitch in the back of Mariah's arm. She was lucky to be alive, Doc Munsey had said more than once.

If the gash had been any deeper the bull would have hit that brachial artery the EMTs referred to earlier and she would have run the risk of bleeding to death.

He pulled in a deep breath and let it out. How was he going to tell her he'd made the decision not to leave her side again?

Someone wanted her to die. Was she safe anywhere? Her home had been violated, public settings were no obstacle to the perpetrator, what was left?

"Why so serious?" she asked, looking up at him

while she hugged the hospital gown to her chest just above her breasts.

A rush of desire surged inside of him as the memory of feeling her skin next to his, flared and burned in his mind.

"There's some SOB out there who wants you dead. Reason enough?"

The slight smile on her lips collapsed, making him regret his words even though they were true. He liked her smiling much better. He liked it when her passion surfaced. He'd like it better if she weren't a cop.

"Can you get police protection?"

"This isn't a rusty episode of *Miami Vice*. I am the protection."

Tension had a stranglehold on his nerves. He had a ranch to run, cattle to herd, spring calves to brand, but his only concern revolved around the woman in front of him. A woman who still didn't trust him. That was something he intended to change.

"You can get dressed, Mariah," Dr. Munsey said, pulling out a prescription pad. "I'll give you some pain medication and an antibiotic. Are you allergic to anything?"

"No."

He scribbled on the pad. "This should work. Remember to keep the wound dry, and consider taking a couple of days off from work. You don't want to tear it open." He ripped the page off and handed it to her, nodded and left the examine room.

Mariah considered the doctor's suggestion for about two seconds. She couldn't leave in the middle of an investigation, and with Baylor's polygraph examination coming up, she'd be remiss if she wasn't there.

An ounce of dread metastasized inside of her. What if he failed the test? There was no one to substantiate his alibi.

"Out…you're keeping me from my duties." She slipped off the examining table and stared at Baylor's retreating backside. An incredible view.

She pulled the curtain, gauging the amount of pain every effort took, even reconsidering Dr. Munsey's suggestion. Her left arm felt like a rock had been taped to it. She attempted to raise it up and away from her body, causing a flash of intense pain that made her gasp.

Good thing she only needed her right hand to fire her pistol. The thought squelched the last of her doubts about being prepared. If she could pull, aim and shoot, she was work ready.

Gingerly she put on the one-armed blouse, and worked the buttons.

Dressed, she shoved the prescription note in the pocket of her jeans and yanked open the bed curtain, only to find Baylor leaning against the wall in an oh-so-sexy stance that made her cheeks flame and her heart rate escalate.

She owed him her life, twice over. How could she ever repay him?

"I've got my pickup outside. I'll take you home."

She liked the sound of that. "Can we hit the pharmacy en route?"

"Sure." He moved out into the hallway and she fell in next to him.

"What would I do without you around to save my butt every time I get into trouble?"

Baylor slowed and stopped. Reaching out, he grasped her good arm. She tried to analyze his face for clues to the tension she could feel coming from his body and radiating into her from his hand.

"Take the day off, Mariah. This is getting out of hand."

Caution stirred inside of her. She tried to relax even while images of Buckner's battered body imploded in her mind.

"I can't take a day off when things get rough, Baylor. There's a madman out there who for some obscure reason wants me dead. Maybe he has Endicott and wants to keep him, maybe someone spit in his cornflakes this morning, but for whatever reason, he's dangerous…to you…to me. I can't quit."

"Detective Ellis." Mariah turned around to find Officer Duffy standing next to her and Baylor.

"I just got a call from Officer Bradshaw. That cowboy, Ray Buckner, he didn't make it. He never regained consciousness." Officer Duffy nodded and left through the main door.

Mariah's heart sagged in her chest and only the feel of Baylor's arms around her kept her from collapsing into a heap on the floor. Her only suspect-witness was dead, along with any information he might have had about why he'd tried to kill them, or who had tried to kill them.

The door opened and CSI Worchester strode in. "Detective Ellis, Officer Duffy said I'd find you here."

Mariah moved toward him. "Yeah, I'm thinking of renting a permanent room. Did you find anything in the bull pen?"

"Contaminated scene. After a dozen Brahmas stomp around in it for hours, there's nothing salvageable, but I'll have more information once Ray Buckner's body is released to the morgue."

"How about the ballistics on the slug from the meadow and Buckner's rifle?"

"Not a match. The bullet wasn't fired from that gun."

Mariah's mouth went dry and a sensation of guilt glided through her body.

What had she done? An innocent man was dead based on her stupid assumption that he'd tried to kill her and Baylor.

"Thanks, Ryan. I'll be in touch."

He left, and she turned back to Baylor.

"Come on, you couldn't know what would happen." He pulled her into his arms. She leaned into him and closed her eyes.

More than anything she wanted to believe that, but she couldn't.

Chapter Seven

"Remove your shirt," the polygraph examiner said, opening his equipment case and hooking up cables.

The interrogation room seemed five times too small to Baylor as he popped the snaps down the front of his plaid shirt and pulled it off.

He knew Mariah was there, just behind the four-by-four square of mirrored glass, watching, hoping…trusting?

"Relax, Mr. McCullough," the examiner said as he placed a band of convoluted rubber tubes around Baylor's chest and abdomen, then cinched them tight.

"Go ahead and have a seat." He gestured to an oversize chair on the opposite side of the table.

Baylor sat down and leaned back, trying to take deep, even breaths to calm his blown nerves. He didn't have anything to hide, save a secret or two, so what were the chances he'd flunk the test?

The polygraph examiner, Wendell Cranston, clamped two small metal plates to the index and pointer fingers of Baylor's right hand, followed by a blood pressure cuff on his left upper arm. He felt like a bovine in a calf roping event, all tied up until the flag dropped.

He watched Wendell plug the leads into a machine that looked something like a seismograph. He tried to breathe normally to combat his growing agitation with the situation he'd volunteered to participate in.

"I'm going to ask a series of exploratory questions which I'll use to form my control questions. The exploratory questions will come off the paperwork you filled out. Do you understand?"

"Yes."

"This machine will record the physiological responses generated by your sympathetic nervous system. These include blood pressure, pulse, respirations and skin conductivity. This machine can detect lies, so it's important to answer my questions truthfully. Do you understand?"

"Yes."

Wendell switched on the machine, its low hum filling the room and further eroding Baylor's resolve.

"Is your name Baylor McCullough?"

"Yes."

"Do you live in Idaho?"

"Yes."

"Are you thirty-four years of age?"

"Yes." Baylor stared straight ahead, feeling the tension in his body ease.

Wendell Cranston stared down at the graph and made several marks on the paper. "I'm going to conduct a stim test now, in which I'll ask you to deliberately tell a lie. Do you understand?"

"Yes."

"Is your name Baylor McCullough?"

"No."

Wendell made a mark on the paper as it flowed out of the machine. "Are you thirty-four years old?"

"No."

"Are you married?"

"Yes." Baylor cleared his throat and sucked in a deep breath, seeing his last images of Amy flash in his mind. "I'm a widower."

"Just yes or no answers, Mr. McCullough."

Baylor shut his eyes and tried to focus on the examiner's voice, but he could feel his muscles clenching tight between his shoulder blades.

"Do you live on the Bellwether Ranch?"

"No."

"Were you born in Idaho?"

"No."

"That concludes the stim test. I was able to detect the lies, and to establish a baseline. We're ready to begin."

Baylor sucked in a deep breath, opened his eyes and glanced at the mirror. What was he thinking? He was doing this for her. Something about the way she saw him mattered on a primal level that he couldn't explain.

"Do you know James Endicott?"

"Yes."

"Did you see James Endicott on April the fifth of this year?"

"No."

"Is your name Baylor McCullough?"

"Yes."

"Did you know James Endicott was having an affair with your wife, Amy?"

"No!"

"Do you live on the Bellwether Ranch?"

"Yes." With all the remaining patience Baylor could muster he remained in the chair, determined to stay put until the bitter end.

"Did you kill James Endicott?"

"No."

"Did you have anything to do with James Endicott's disappearance?"

"No."

"Were you born in Idaho?"

"Yes."

"Do you know the whereabouts of James Endicott?"

"No."

"Are you thirty-four years of age?"

"Yes."

MARIAH STOOD FROZEN in front of the mirrored window, staring at Baylor. She could see the tense set of his shoulders, hear the stress in his voice. Had she done the right thing, asking him to take a polygraph? And what if he didn't pass? Was she prepared to deal with that?

She hit the off button on the open microphone and the viewing room went silent. It was easier that way. She'd lost every ounce of her objectivity in this case. It was time to give it up. Time to let go. But could she step out on him now?

Her throat tightened, reality twisted around her thoughts and she pondered the real question. Could she bear to never see him again?

The viewing-room door banged open and Ted Ellis strode in, closing the door behind him.

"Has he cracked yet?"

"No, Dad, but any moment now." She'd been unable to keep the sarcasm from lacing itself around her words, a fact that her father jumped on.

"I've been watching you, Mariah, and you've gone gaga on McCullough." Ted Ellis glanced at his wristwatch. "You've got until five o'clock this afternoon to pull yourself together or you're off this case."

She wheeled on her father, but couldn't find the words to rebut. A sense of calm settled over her as she glanced down at her watch. "Only three hours to go. Thank you, and I'll take a couple of days off while I'm at it."

For the first time in forever, Chief Ellis was speechless, but it didn't take him long to find his tongue. "You really have lost your objectivity, haven't you?"

Turning back to the glass, she watched Wendell Cranston release Baylor.

Her mouth went dry and she mentally traced every hard line of his broad chest. A rush of need spiked in her veins. "Yes, I have. He's a decent man and I owe him my life."

Mariah's throat tightened; the admission was cathartic. "I believe he's innocent."

Her father stared at her and shook his head. "Let me know when you're ready. I'll reassign the case to Maxwell, and if he can't catch a break, the feds are next in line."

A shudder skimmed her body. The idea of turning over jurisdiction to the FBI didn't sit well. "I plan to wait for the examiner's report before I make my decision."

"I wouldn't want it any other way." Her dad patted her shoulder. "I've always encouraged you to follow your gut, Mariah. That's what put you on his trail in the first place, but sometimes your feelings get in the way of your gut and you have to accept that."

Dread bubbled up inside of her and she turned back to the viewing window. She didn't know what to think anymore.

"Point taken."

Cranston gave the wrap sign, holding up four fingers on his right hand. She watched Baylor pull on his shirt and work the snaps before he pushed his hat down low on his head and left the room.

"Do you want me to stay for the analysis?"

"No. I can take whatever Wendell has to say."

"Okay." Her dad left the viewing room and she continued to watch the examiner as he studied the roll of graph paper, marking it at random intervals.

Her heart pounded in her eardrums. She could feel the tension as it agitated her muscles one by one until she thought she'd explode if she waited any longer.

Wendell waved his hand for her to come into the room and she exited the viewing room, working hard to keep her steps as casual as possible.

Baylor stood in the hallway, tall and relaxed, like a man without a problem in the world.

Her steps faltered, and she came face-to-face with him. "I hope it's everything you need, Mariah."

The low sexy quality of his voice was as effective as a caress, and she fought the urge to lean into him. To feel his arms around her.

"I only need the truth." She gazed up at him and for an instant his eyes narrowed.

"I'm not sure you could handle it."

"Try me."

Contemplation played on his features. He was a man teetering between two options, the truth or a lie. Rattled, she suddenly didn't want either tossed her way. Not from him, not right now. "Save it until after I've gotten Wendell's analysis. We might have lots more to talk about by then."

He didn't comment as she turned away, a fact that

bothered her. She entered the interrogation room and closed the door behind her. What was he hiding?

"Detective." Wendell reached out and shook her hand.

"Did you arrive at a conclusion?" Anticipation poised her nerves on the edge of an emotional precipice.

"Yes."

BAYLOR PACED THE corridor, feeling every second pass in torturous increments. He'd told the truth, answered the questions Wendell had put to him. Why didn't he feel like the outcome would say otherwise?

He sat down in one of the chairs that lined the hallway. He needed to tell Mariah about the night Amy died. He was sure she'd already read the file— what good detective wouldn't? An edge of guilt sliced into him, releasing a flood of emotions he'd believed he'd dealt with.

The interrogation-room door opened and Mariah stepped out, followed by Wendell Cranston and his black suitcase of lie detector paraphernalia. He turned left and disappeared into the station.

Baylor stood up, trying to gauge the look on Mariah's face, but got nothing. Caution hedged his bet on the outcome, and a pang of anxiety chased through him.

"Put me out of my misery," he said, glad when she finally looked him in the eye.

"Wendell ruled it inconclusive. Your answer spikes to the control questions match your answer spikes to the relevant questions. You're either a fabulous liar, or the most truthful suspect I've ever met."

He didn't know whether to demand a retake or be content with inconclusive. Either way he was back at square one with her. He reached out and grasped her elbow, steering her toward the door. He needed her alone, needed to touch her, to coax her, to make her understand, to make her believe, but she stopped short and pulled out of his grasp.

"The odds are pretty good I'll be pulled off this case by morning."

Caution settled around his nerves and he suddenly understood why she'd been so hopeful that the polygraph would produce a positive result. "I'll be bait for the next detective who'd like nothing better than to prove I had something to do with Endicott's disappearance?"

The downcast glance of her eyes told him he was spot-on. "Is this your choice, Mariah?"

She looked straight at him and his heart slammed against his ribs.

"I've lost my objectivity…" her voice dropped to a whisper "…where you're concerned. I can't do my job when I'm around you."

Desire, hot and all consuming, ignited in his body and he reached out for her. She didn't resist, but took his hand and steered him across the hall into the viewing room. The door shut and he heard the lock engage. Gone were the last of the emotional restraints that boxed him in. He knew at that moment she felt the fire, too. Experienced the primal burn of need heating them to white-hot.

Mariah's breath caught in her throat. She focused on the feel of Baylor's hands moving over her body with slow seductive precision. Everywhere he touched he left her skin humming with the need for more.

She raised her mouth to his and he pinned her to the door with his body. It was crazy, it was sane, it was everything in between, and she needed him like she needed air. She breathed him in, trying to reconcile her emotions with her primal physical response to his heated touch. A small sigh escaped from her as he deepened the kiss, demanding more without words.

The thud of rushed footsteps in the hall outside of the viewing room pulled her from the lust-induced haze, and she ended the kiss.

Baylor groaned.

"Did you hear that?" she asked, reluctantly stepping back from him and smoothing her hair.

His eyes had darkened and still smoldered with a desire so palpable she felt like she could reach out and touch it, or bring it back to life in an instant.

Three loud raps on the door sounded and echoed in the tiny room. Baylor moved in front of the mirrored glass and leaned against it, crossing his arms over his chest.

Mariah pulled open the door, spotting a uniformed officer as he was poised to enter the interrogation room.

"What's going on?"

"Dispatch just got a couple of 911 calls for the rural fire department. There's a structure fire on the Bellwether Ranch."

Panic zipped through her as she pulled the door all the way open and stepped out into the corridor with Baylor on her heels.

"Did they say what kind of structure?" she asked.

"A barn, I think. I thought McCullough should know." The officer headed back toward the station.

Baylor pushed past her and headed for the door. It took everything he had not to run.

Fires in the backcountry were hard to fight. There were no hydrants to hook onto. The water would have to be trucked in, in a tanker that usually arrived after the structure had been reduced to ashes. Already he was counting his losses. Thankfully he'd turned the horses out this morning and the band of calves who'd been rescued from the storm were back with their mothers in the pasture.

"I've got to go," he said over his shoulder as he pushed out into the afternoon sun. Then he bolted, leaving the afterglow of kissing Mariah in his wake, but not completely out of mind.

DUSK HAD DESCENDED on the high country when he roared up the driveway two hours later. The haze of smoke had been visible in the air by the time he'd left the Salmon River road and crossed onto Bell-wether property.

He braked hard and stared at the blackened skeleton of the barn that had been standing on the ranch since before he was born. A couple of two-ton bales of hay still flamed out, despite the fireman holding the water hose on it.

Two water tender tankers covered the scene along with a dozen volunteer firemen, and Travis, his ranch hand, sat on the back bumper of one of the trucks with his head down.

Worry stewed inside of Baylor. Was Travis okay? He pulled in a breath and climbed out of his pickup. He'd mentally prepared for the worst. At least none of his livestock had perished in the fire.

He strode over to Travis, seeing the soot on his face and the regret in his eyes as he stood up. "I tried to put it out, but it got so big."

Baylor put his hand on the kid's back. "Are you okay?"

"Yeah."

"That's all that matters. The barn can be replaced. You can't. Head in and get cleaned up."

Travis nodded and took off for the bunkhouse situated a hundred feet behind the barn.

"McCullough." The rural fire chief raised his hand and strode over to Baylor's side. "We tried to save the old girl, your ranch hand got some water on the fire, but it blew up. We couldn't get here in time."

"Thanks, Jock. I know you all did your best."

The sound of gravel crunching beneath tires drew his attention to the driveway, where he spotted Mariah's car pulling in next to his pickup.

"Any idea where it started?" he asked the fire chief, while he studied her moving toward them.

"The point of origin is in the southern corner. What did you have back there?"

"A calf warming pen." Baylor mentally went through his routine, certain he'd unplugged every last heat lamp. Caution perked in his veins. Barn fires weren't uncommon. There were a couple a year within the county. Usually caused by lightning, or hot equipment being parked on hay-littered floorboards.

"When can we get in there for a good look?"

"Maybe in an hour or so. It's still too hot right now."

Mariah came to stand next to him and he put his hand on her back. "I'm going inside, Jock. If you or your men need anything, you're welcome to it. Let me know when you investigate where the fire started."

"No problem. Thanks, Baylor." Jock Hansen turned and moved back toward his fire crew.

"It's just wood. I'll rebuild. Now, where were we?" He felt Mariah hesitate and looked over at her.

"I can't believe we were kissing in the station. My dad would have a fit." She smiled and he stared at her lips, feeling his desire ratchet up.

"It would be just a short hop into a cell from there. Maybe it's the safest place to kiss you." He liked the way her cheeks pinked up and her blue eyes sparkled in the low light.

Every throbbing inch of him wanted her, but he held back from a full-on pursuit, restrained by his own sense of guilt. Did it matter whether or not he told her the truth about the night Amy died?

"Want something to drink?" He moved her toward the front door.

"Yeah. Sounds like it's going to be a long night."

"Hay bales can smolder for weeks. They'll have to let them burn out by themselves." Baylor pulled his house key out and reached for the knob. It turned in his hand.

"Weird."

"What?"

"I locked this door this morning."

"Like you turned off the heat lamp in the barn?"

"Yeah. Stay here. I'm going to check it out."

He was glad when she didn't put up a protest, pull her gun and charge in. This was his territory.

The house was dead quiet, but he listened anyway. Semidarkness filled the rooms and he reached for the light switch next to the door, flipping it on.

Baylor took several steps into the living room, satisfied everything was in its place, but an odd scent greeted him as he stepped into the kitchen.

Gasoline. Just a hint, like someone had it on their clothes as they moved through the house.

Caution worked through him, but he wasn't ready to make a call like that until after the point of origin had been determined by Jock. If the same person who started the barn fire had been in his home, why in the hell hadn't he torched it, too?

"Baylor?"

The sound of Mariah's voice brought him around and he tried to look relaxed even though he didn't feel it. "In the kitchen."

He flipped on the light, pulled a couple of tall glasses out of the cupboard and opened the refrigerator door, spotting the glass pitcher of iced tea he'd put there that morning.

"Damn, would you look at that?" He pulled the container out of the fridge and held it up to the kitchen light.

Clearly outlined in the bottom of the pitcher was a gun. A 357, if he guessed right.

His 357.

"I'd rather have ice in mine," Mariah said, staring at the container. Uncertainty quaked through her as she searched Baylor's face for an explanation.

"It wasn't there this morning, but the front door was unlocked when we got here."

"Why would anyone hide a gun…unless it was used in the commission of a crime."

"Do you have a paper bag?"

He set the pitcher down on the counter, took a brown bag out of the pantry and handed it to her.

Mariah pulled her pen out of her pocket and fished in the container, catching the loop behind the trigger. Carefully she raised the gun up out of the tea and let it drain before slipping it inside the bag to turn over to the lab.

A sense of foreboding latched on to her nerves. She had no proof Baylor hadn't put it there, only a gut feeling.

A loud knock dragged her attention away and she followed him out of the kitchen and into the living room, where he opened the front door.

"She's cooled down enough that we can get inside. We won't be poking around, it's still too hot, but we can find a point of origin." Jock Hansen led them outside and toward the barn to an area where two huge floodlights had been staged.

"Watch your step, there are still hot spots." He turned on his flashlight and moved into the barn.

Mariah's toes curled up in her shoes as she stepped into the blackened structure anticipating a trip over the hot coals that glowed on the floor all around her.

The inside was a hollow cavern shrouded in darkness and barely lit up by the bright lights. Charred boards told the story of the barn's layout and she tried to imagine it with the stalls and hayloft still intact.

Gingerly she followed along next to Baylor.

"This looks like the place where it started." Jock indicated a corner pen about twenty feet long and twenty feet wide. "The heat lamps are melted, but you can see the outline of the one lying on the floor."

Mariah strained to see it, but finally made out the lines of the melted lamp.

"The fire started in the dry bedding on the floor." Jock shined his flashlight beam on the charred boards, illuminating the fan pattern where the fire had progressed. "Then it caught the wall on fire." He eased the light up a foot at a time as he explained the fire science.

"Then it…" A half-choked yell rattled out of Jock's throat and he launched backward, his flashlight beam aimed toward the ceiling. "Son-of-a-bitch."

Mariah felt a wave of nausea sweep over her as she, too, stepped back and stared up at the roof.

There, swinging back and forth on a cable in the night breeze was a body, or a least what was left of one.

Baylor caught her before she could lean any farther back.

"I've got to phone this in immediately." She turned in his arms.

"You won't get any argument from me," he said.

Her features were unreadable in the dim lighting, but he felt her go stiff in his arms. Was it possible the charred body swaying in the breeze belonged to James Endicott?

A sickening reality settled over him as he let her go and watched her jog out of the barn.

Not even passing a polygraph was going to convince her he had nothing to do with this. That was if he ever got the chance to take another one.

"I think this burned-out shell just became a crime scene. Maybe you better pull your guys out before any more evidence is destroyed."

Jock nodded in agreement, and retreated.

Baylor stayed put, searching for any clues that might help him, but he saw nothing. Nothing but a pile of ashes and more questions than answers.

Chapter Eight

Exhaustion cramped Mariah's muscles as she watched dawn break over the mountain and the sun's first rays stream through the pines next to the barn.

Baylor had made himself scarce since the crime scene techs had rolled up on scene three hours earlier, and she found herself worrying more about him than the implications of the body hanging in his torched barn.

Maybe it wasn't James Endicott. Maybe… She rubbed her temples, sure the headache would pass if she drank another cup of coffee.

"We're ready to drop the body," CSI Worchester said, moving toward her. "The fire destroyed any evidence that might have otherwise been there. We looked for fiber evidence on the cable, got something. It'll probably match with McCullough's gloves. The only thing we've got left is the body."

"Thanks, Ryan." She paused in the entrance of the barn and watched them spread out a plastic sheet, then cover it with a sterile drape in the area where the body would touch down.

A knot formed in her stomach, a mix of nerves and anticipation. She prayed there was some sort of trace on the corpse. Anything that would lead her investigation away from Baylor. Anything at all. But the circumstantial evidence was beginning to mount and she wasn't sure it wouldn't eventually produce an avalanche.

The clack of the teeth on the ratchet wench set her mind on edge. She watched as the charred body was lowered. Could Baylor really do something heinous like this? She searched her heart, digging for the knowledge, and finding it locked inside. Baylor was an honorable man.

Ryan, dressed in a clean suit, face shield and gloves, steered the body the last six feet, making sure it was positioned in the middle of the sheet.

Mariah stepped closer, careful to stay outside of the clean perimeter. The evidence Ryan recovered could make the difference between Baylor being cleared and… She couldn't force her thoughts to go there. In spite of all of her training, in spite of her years as a cop and finally a detective. It all turned to a jumble when she thought about him.

"Drama and trauma," Ryan said as he took a pair of bolt cutters from one of his technicians and prepared to cut the cable in order to free the body for transport.

"Everyone, watch yourselves. These cables can do some crazy things." He set the bolt cutters three feet from the point where the cable had been placed around the neck of the corpse and clamped down.

The cable snipped and coiled in midair as the tension was released, springing up toward the ceiling of the barn before relaxing to swing ten feet above their heads.

Ryan handed the bolt cutters back to his waiting tech. "Get Detective Ellis a mask."

Mariah was handed a cup-style surgical mask and an eye shield. She put them on and stepped closer.

Already, Ryan was examining the body. "The victim appears to be male. Approximate age…late thirties."

Every muscle in her body cranked tighter as Ryan went on. He was describing James Endicott. If only the fire hadn't burned away any distinguishing facial features.

"That's odd."

Her hearing tuned up. "You've got something?"

"I'm not sure. Jenny, I need a liver temp probe."

Mariah looked away the moment the tech put the instrument in Ryan's hand. The forensic end of her job had a tendency to turn her stomach inside out.

"Strange."

Taking a deep breath, she looked back at the scene and put her professional face on. "What?"

"His liver temp is…well, it's forty degrees. That's impossible."

Mariah calculated what the temperature had been yesterday, and overnight, both temps well above forty degrees. "What about the fire? That should have raised the temperature."

"You'd think. Unless…he started out really, really cold."

"Frozen?" Curiosity coiled around her thought processes. "That would explain why his body temperature is less than the outside air temperature."

"The average household freezer maintains a temperature of zero to minus ten. If he was that cold in the beginning, that would explain why the fire charred his skin, but didn't destroy the subcutaneous fat layers underneath."

"Any signs of cause of death?"

"Well, we know he didn't die in the fire." Ryan stood up from his squatting position next to the body. "I'm going to need time in the morgue before I can give you anything else. We'll X-ray for foreign bodies, and take dental slides. Do you think this is James Endicott, your missing prosecutor?"

"Yeah, I do, but let's keep it under wraps until we get a positive I.D."

"You've got it." Ryan waved his tech over and together they began lapping the sheet over the body, preparing it for transport to the county morgue.

Did Baylor have a freezer? She didn't recall seeing one. A measure of relief surged through her as she left the barn.

"Is it him?"

The question came at her from out of the shadows shrouding the left side of the barn.

Mariah stopped and turned to face Baylor. His features were chiseled into hard lines. He looked like he hadn't slept in days. His hat was pulled low, but she could still see his blue-gray eyes under the brim of his Stetson.

Her brain worked double time as she bounced between two extremes. Guilty, not guilty.

"We can't make a positive I.D. until Ryan gets the body to the morgue for analysis—"

"Cut the company line, Mariah." He stepped toward her and she automatically closed her eyes, expecting to feel the gentle touch of his hand on her skin, but the fantasy didn't materialize.

She opened her lids and gazed up at him.

Tension ticked along his jawline, his eyes narrowing as he studied her. "It's him, isn't it?" His teeth clamped together.

"I think so." She wanted to implode as she watched a mix of anger, resentment and resignation flow over his features. "Let's wait it out, Baylor. There's always a chance it's not him." The words tasted like fluff. A hope cooked to half-baked.

"I was taking a polygraph when this happened." He motioned to the scorched barn. "You're my alibi."

"You could have used some sort of light timer to activate the heat lamp hours before the fire started."

He glared at her, shaking his head in disbelief. "And I booked a seat on the next damn shuttle to Mars."

Mariah swallowed. "Do you have a freezer?"

"What?"

"A freezer, Baylor. A chest freezer." Her throat tightened and every nerve in her body twisted tight. She'd rather be anywhere than here. Rather be kissing him than shaking him down for murder.

"Yeah. It's in the garage. But what the hell does a freezer—" The end of Baylor's sentence caught in his throat as he put the puzzle together. "I'm going in the house to call my lawyer." He took a step back from her, when all he wanted to do was take her in his arms and hold her.

He could see the pain in her eyes, feel her internal struggle, but she was a cop. At the moment, her obligation was to her badge.

The sound of tires on gravel pulled his attention to a red BMW, hauling ass up the driveway. It ground to a stop in a cloud of dust. A woman bailed out of the car and headed straight for them.

"Detective Ellis. Where is he? Where's my husband? I heard the call come in over the police scanner."

Caution took hold of Mariah's actions as she sized up Rachel Endicott. The woman had been on her back since she'd reported James missing. But she'd probably have done the same, only there was something off about her emotionless rants every couple of days.

"Mrs. Endicott, we're not even sure it's him at this

point. Go home. I'll contact you as soon as I've got a positive I.D."

"I won't leave! I want to see my husband's body." Her face went red with anger and exertion. She turned toward Baylor, warning Mariah that she intended to confront him next. "Did you kill him?" she asked, glaring at Baylor.

"No." He took a step toward her. "I'm sorry, Mrs. Endicott. Sorry for your loss."

Rachel Endicott's eyes went wide and for a moment Mariah thought the woman was going to burst into tears, but she got a hold of herself and took a step back.

"I'm sorry, Detective. You know how to reach me." She dropped her gaze to the ground and turned around, walked back to her car, climbed in and backed down the driveway.

Mariah tried to relax but she couldn't shake the odd sensation combing up and down her spine. Rachel Endicott had been acting strange since the moment her philandering husband had vanished. Did she know about the affair between James and Amy McCullough?

"I'd say she was a blip on your radar," Baylor said from next to her.

"Not exactly a grieving widow." In fact, Rachel Endicott had never really struck her that way, now that Mariah considered her meetings with the woman.

"Everyone handles loss differently. No one

knows what goes on behind closed doors. Maybe she was ready to divorce the cheating bastard when he disappeared."

Mariah tossed Baylor a suspicious glance. "And how would you know that?"

"If Endicott didn't have the character to be a one-woman man, do you think Amy was the only woman he played around with, the only marriage he destroyed?"

Mariah tried to dissipate his argument, to chalk it up to bitterness, but she couldn't. Baylor was right. Men like James Endicott dabbled at their own risk and it was hard to tell whom they'd angered in the process.

"Did he really crush your marriage to Amy?" The question was personal and probing, but somewhere in her heart she needed to hear the answer.

"No. What Amy and I had was gone long before Endicott took her physically from me. Amy was looking for a way out from the day we married. I'm surprised she said I do."

Somewhere in her soul, Mariah felt a shift. She'd always felt guilty for kissing Baylor. Always felt like some sort of husband stealer for wanting him.

"Amy always planned to take off for L.A. the minute she graduated from high school. She was going to be a star," Mariah said, reliving the memory of exuberance Amy had always used to paint her world.

"I wasn't what she wanted, Mariah. I never was. The Bellwether was a prison in her mind. All the

fresh air and open country made her feel trapped."
He shook his head, accentuating his disbelief.

She saw the tension around his eyes soften.

"She planned to leave. I asked her to get on with
it. We needed to move forward. I didn't hold her. She
was free to go."

Surprise laced through Mariah, catching her in a
net of curiosity. "What happened?"

"The night she died, we had dinner at the Steak
House Restaurant in town. We'd agreed to separate
months before that, but for some reason she stayed
put. Money maybe, I don't know."

The air charged with a feeling of sadness Mariah
couldn't shake. Had Amy planned to run off with
James Endicott?

"We argued just before we left in her car."

"She was driving. That's what the eyewitness said
and it's why the vehicular manslaughter charges Endicott brought against you were dropped."

A faraway stare seemed to pull Baylor away from
her and back into the past. She watched him swallow
hard, sensing an internal struggle churning inside of
him. Was he reliving that horrific night one terrible
moment at a time?

"That's not what happened."

Her heart slammed against her rib cage and she
sucked in a labored breath. She suddenly didn't want
him to go on, didn't want to know the truth.

"Amy wasn't driving. I was. I made her pull over

on the edge of town and I took over." He reached for her and she felt his hand on her elbow. Her skin tingled beneath his fingers and she resisted the urge to touch his cheek, to soothe away the pain she could see in his eyes as he stared down at her.

"It happened so fast, I couldn't stop it. The deer jumped out of the ditch. I jerked the steering wheel to the left to avoid it, but the car pulled to the right. For some damn reason it all went to hell in a hand basket, and we were in the river…the car filled with water. I couldn't get her to talk to me."

Mariah's throat squeezed shut, her eyes stinging as she blinked back tears. Baylor's words painted a vivid picture of the terror they'd experienced in the cold, dark water, of the panic and struggle he'd gone through only to lose her.

"Her seat belt jammed, but I yanked it free. She was conscious, but dazed. I kicked out the driver's-side window and floated out. I never should have left her."

Baylor felt his chest tighten until he was sure he couldn't take another breath. He stared into Mariah's eyes, looking for a hint of skepticism, a trace of disbelief, and then he realized she was crying. Reaching out to touch her cheek, he brushed away her tears.

"I couldn't swim. I had a hold of her for an instant. Dammit! I couldn't save her. I barely saved myself. If I hadn't found a rock under the water to hold on to, I'd have been swept away."

Then she was holding him, stroking his cheek with her hand. Baylor buried his face in her hair, breathing her in with desperate gulps of air.

The truth was out. He was free. All that mattered now was protecting the woman in his arms from a madman crazy enough to try to take her away.

MARIAH SIFTED THROUGH her copies of the crime scene photos one more time before moving on to the autopsy report. She'd managed to keep the case, but she knew Chief Ellis wasn't going to allow it for much longer unless she could fork over some solid proof.

She was convinced Baylor had been set up for Endicott's murder, right down to the gun in the tea pitcher, which had produced a ballistics match for the single slug in Endicott's right temple. The gunshot wound was his cause of death, but the freezer angle still gave her pause.

Worchester hadn't been able to establish a time of death, but it could have been weeks before the fire.

Someone had intentionally waylaid the discovery of Endicott's body. But why?

"Give it a rest, Mariah. Eat." Baylor slid a plate of food in front of her and she gave him a smile.

"Thank you, but I've got to figure out what I'm missing."

"It'll wait." He took her hand and pulled her off her stool at the bar separating her dining room and kitchen. He was gorgeous, she thought as she stepped into his open arms and raised her mouth to his.

She was risking it all, having him here, but he was a persuasive man, with his caution and certainty that she was in danger, and that he was the only one who could provide her with the protection she needed. She needed something from him all right.

Stretching up onto her tiptoes, she brushed her lips against his. Warmth spread throughout her body and put her case on hold. She was off-duty. It was the weekend.

"Um." He pulled back, staring down at her with a seductive smile that made her heart flutter.

"Dessert?"

"What did you have in mind?" she asked.

"A banana split down at Ruby's Diner."

"My favorite." She kissed him again and turned for the front door, feeling like a teenager about to embark on her first date.

"I remember saving my babysitting money for those, and movies at the Roxy Theater." She grabbed her house key and slid it into the pocket of her jeans, lost in the snippet of nostalgia that went with a small-town Saturday night.

She stepped through the door with Baylor behind her and moseyed down the steps in the late evening twilight. Somewhere down the street a dog barked. The scent of lilacs hung in the air, along with a smell she didn't recognize. She turned at the gate and watched him stride down the path toward her, his hat pulled low, his sultry gaze locked on her, as if she were the only woman on the planet.

The smell reached his nose seconds before he heard the hissing noise.

Terror launched him forward as the natural gas ignited. He lunged for Mariah.

Slamming into her, he took her to the ground, covering her with his body.

Tongues of fire lashed out and roared over their heads, raining heat and fiery debris down on them.

They had to move or risk being burned.

"Can you walk?" he said into her ear.

"Yeah."

He pulled Mariah to her feet and kicked the front gate open where it hung from a single hinge. Holding her next to him, he hurried across the street and away from the flames now shooting out of the roof of her house.

He heard the whine of a siren in the distance.

Baylor didn't stop moving until they reached a wide expanse of grass in a neighbor's front yard across the street.

Gently he lowered her to the ground and sat down next to her, brushing the blackened debris out of her hair.

"Saved by a banana split." His attempt at humor didn't erase the look of distress that pulled her eyebrows together and marred her beautiful face. He didn't like the way she guarded her right arm against her body. She needed medical attention.

He glanced at the acrid black smoke rolling out of the roof into the air. Neighbors stood in the street and on the sidewalks watching the action, as a couple of fire engines pulled up on scene and firemen scrambled to douse the flames before they ignited the homes on either side of Mariah's.

"What happened?"

"You didn't smell the gas when you came outside?"

"No…I was preoccupied."

"With the case. Dammit, Mariah. You have to listen to me. Someone wants you dead. This wasn't an accident." Frustration stirred in his body. What more proof did she need, and what happened if he wasn't there to protect her the next time?

"You need to dump this case. Turn it over to someone else before you get hurt." *Or worse.* He searched her face for some hint that his words were sinking into her brain, disappointed when she shook her head.

"Detective Maxwell is next in line, Baylor. He'll take you apart…put you in—"

"Stop, Mariah." He brushed his hand against her cheek. "You don't have to protect me. I haven't done anything wrong. Let me protect you. Come to the Bellwether."

Mariah's mouth went dry as she stared into Baylor's eyes and gave his proposition a chance to sink in. If only things were different. If she weren't a cop and him her suspect, if life were normal and…

"I can't. Not like this." She looked away and stared at what was left of her home as the firemen attempted to put out the fire. "My career is in shambles, and now my home, too. I can't make a decision like that right now."

With his hand he pulled her chin around, forcing her to meet his gaze. "This nutcase isn't going to stop. Let me help you figure out who he is and what he wants, before he manages to kill us both."

His reasoning worked its way into her brain, finding a measure of acceptance there. They were both walking targets for some reason and until they caught the creep turning their world upside down they couldn't have a world…not together anyway. Realization clung to her thoughts. She was falling hard for Baylor McCullough.

"I have an interview with Rachel Endicott first thing Monday morning. I can't let go of this case until I've had a chance to talk to her. She knows something."

Baylor leaned closer. "Judging by her weird appearance at the ranch, yeah. She could have taken the pictures of Amy and her husband together."

"Maybe, if she knew about the affair and wanted to catch him in the act, get a better divorce settlement. Could be what she felt went beyond jealousy. Maybe *she* killed him."

Pain shot through Mariah's forearm and clear up into her shoulder, causing her to suck in a labored breath.

"What is it?" Concern played across Baylor's face.

"My arm. I think it's broken."

Baylor stood up, spotting an ambulance as it pulled in just up the block. "Stay put, I'm going to get help."

He moved into the street and waved for the EMS crew, who came running with their jump kit.

"What have you got?"

"Over here. I think she has a broken arm."

They followed him onto the lawn and he stepped back while they assessed Mariah's injuries.

Baylor searched the faces of the gathered crowd, fighting the sensation of being watched. Granted there were a ton of rubbernecking neighbors spurred by curiosity, but he couldn't help feeling like the perpetrator of the explosion was there, watching, obsessing and planning to do it again, only with fatal results the next time.

"We're going to transport her. The doc will have to set and cast her arm."

Baylor dropped his search-and-destroy mode and watched them help Mariah to her feet.

She shook her head when they attempted to put

her on the gurney. "I can't lie down, it hurts too much. I'll walk."

Baylor fell in behind the group as they steadied her and helped her to the ambulance. Taking one last look at the scene, he climbed in for the ride to the hospital.

MARIAH SHUDDERED IN the darkness as she stood next to Baylor, trying to get used to the feel of the newly formed cast on her broken wrist. It was late, she was exhausted and she smelled like a chimney, but she wanted to know what had triggered the explosion at her house.

Baylor put his arm around her, and she absorbed the heat coming from his body, letting it calm her insides.

She focused on the spot where Fire Chief Bill Higgins shined his flashlight next to the outside wall of what was once her home.

"This gas meter blew. I'll have to get the ATF in here to verify my findings, but it looks like it was rigged with some kind of a detonator." He pointed out the pipe where the gas used to come into the house. It looked like an open flower with jagged petals.

She leaned into Baylor, drawing comfort from the feel of his protective presence. He'd managed to save her again. Maybe the third time really was the charm.

"Keep me posted. I'm sure my insurance company will be in touch."

"No problem. I'll make the call to ATF." Bill Higgins moved away from them and headed for his truck.

"Where will you go?" Baylor asked as he turned her toward the sidewalk, stepping over the hose that had been used to save everything around her house, including his pickup.

"I'm going to my dad's place for a while. After that, I'm not sure."

He pulled her up short next to the truck, and lifted her chin with his fingers. Damn, her eyes were blue in the streetlight, and he wanted to taste her mouth in the worst way.

"My offer stands, just say the word."

A smile bowed her lips. "I can't make a decision right now."

Baylor released her, opened the pickup door and helped her inside.

He took one last look at her demolished house before sliding in behind the steering wheel.

Mariah wasn't safe in this town and there was only one place where he could protect her.

The Bellwether Ranch.

Chapter Nine

Mariah tried to relax where she stood in the viewing room with her father, waiting for Rachel Endicott and her lawyer to show up.

On her right arm, just below her elbow, she sported a neon-pink, glow-in-the-dark cast. She wiggled her exposed fingers as much out of nervousness as to make sure blood still flowed into them.

"I need a leave of absence, Dad."

"I'll sign off on one month. That should be enough time to get your arm healed and your pen hand working again."

She'd made her decision not long after Baylor had asked her to come to the Bellwether. She didn't know what the option would bring, but she planned to follow her heart.

"I'm not sure a month is enough. I'm thinking about resigning from the department."

Ted Ellis's eyes widened. "You're going to throw away your career and your badge? For what? Because one damn case is kicking your tail down the street?"

"No. Because this is your career choice for me. You pushed me and I didn't push back. I never got the chance to explore what I wanted to do with my life."

Her father was silent, a fact that helped calm her frazzled nerves. She'd seen too much in this line of work, and she knew somewhere under all the dregs, she had to expose her true passion. Art.

The door to the interrogation room opened and Rachel Endicott trooped in with her lawyer behind her. They pulled out chairs on the same side of the table and sat down.

"If that's really what you want, Mariah, I'll start the paperwork."

She stared at her father. He was gruff, he was intimidating, but under his rough exterior, he understood.

"Thanks."

"Better get going after your last interview before I turn this case over to Detective Maxwell. He's been chomping at the bit for weeks. Tapes rolling on this interview."

A zing of concern laced through her. Giving up the case was going to put Baylor in Maxwell's crosshairs. She dodged a moment of anxiety and left the viewing room.

Mariah sucked in a couple of deep breaths and clutched the case file a little tighter in her left hand.

She knew Baylor was innocent until proven guilty, but he lounged in purgatory between the two opposites. Maybe Rachel Endicott was his ticket out and it was Mariah's job to expose the truth.

She shifted the file to her right fingertips and opened the door with her left hand. Awkward but effective.

"Mrs. Endicott. Mr. Pruett." Mariah laid the file on the table, pulled out her chair and sat down. She opened the folder and put the pictures out in front of Rachel, gauging her reaction. She didn't flinch, just stared at the photos calmly before looking up.

"You knew about your husband's affair with Amy McCullough?"

Rachel glanced at her lawyer, then back at Mariah before answering the question.

"Yes. I knew about it." She swallowed, her eyes luminous with tears. She blinked the tears away. "After everything I did for that bastard. I put him through law school, gave up my own career so he could thrive, and that's what I get in return." She slammed her hand down on the snapshots.

"So you killed him?"

Rachel's face contorted with anger. "No! If I'd done it, I'd have skipped putting the cable around his scrawny neck, and gone straight for his—"

"Rachel. Keep to the specific questions." Deiter Pruett patted his client's hand.

Just when it was getting interesting, Mariah

thought as she shuffled the bagged pictures into a pile with her good hand.

"So you hired a private investigator to take these shots?" she asked, studying Rachel's face.

"No. I didn't."

Mariah paused, staring at her as caution leaked into her veins. "Did you take them yourself?"

"No."

"You had nothing to do with turning them over to the department?"

"No."

What was Rachel hiding? It was clear she'd seen the pictures before. Her reaction, or lack of one, had given her away. "Have you seen these before?"

Rachel's lips pulled into a straight line and she looked over at Deiter Pruett.

Mariah leaned forward and put her arms on the table in front of her, knowing the interview was over.

Rachel Endicott wasn't going to budge an inch.

"My client refuses to answer any more of your questions, Detective Ellis. Without a subpoena." Deiter picked up his briefcase from the floor next to him and stood up, helping Rachel out of her chair.

"One more thing," Mariah said, sliding her chair back and coming to her feet to meet Rachel eye to eye.

"You were the last person to see your husband alive on April fifth. That was a Saturday. Court wasn't in session. Did he tell you where he was going?"

"No." Rachel gave her a downcast glance and brushed past, but Mariah was sure she'd seen a wary flash in the woman's dark eyes. She knew something.

"Don't leave town, Mrs. Endicott."

Together the pair left the interrogation room and Mariah sat back down in her chair.

Rachel Endicott was a good liar, but her body language didn't match her story. It would take some concrete evidence and a grand jury to pull a subpoena, neither of which she had.

The door opened and her father stepped into the room, breaking her chain of thought.

"I'll talk to the prosecutor, give him everything we have, which doesn't amount to a whole hill of beans, but we need to find out what she's hiding."

"I'm betting she has seen the photos before. They're not exactly cutesy pics of the family. They're shots you'd use to hurt somebody."

"Blackmail?" her dad asked, taking the chair across from her.

"Maybe. But who would blackmail her, and why? Amy McCullough is dead. James Endicott is dead. There aren't any more viable players in the mix."

"I'll approach the prosecutor, see if we can cut some kind of an immunity deal if she'll tell us what she knows."

"I like it. Do what you have to do." Mariah scooped up the file and stood.

"Do you still want out?" Her father studied her face.

"Yeah. I'm going to take a one-month leave of absence. But you'll keep me in the loop?"

Disappointment pulled his features down. "You'll be the first to know if she takes the deal."

"Thanks, Dad." Mariah made an awkward attempt to hug her father with her good arm. "I'll stay in touch."

"Am I going to have to guess where you're going since your permanent address is no longer habitable?"

"I'm going to follow my heart for a change." She handed her father the case file and pulled open the door, stepping out into the corridor, fixated on reaching Baylor and the Bellwether Ranch as soon as possible. She didn't even need to pack. A suspicious gas leak had taken care of that, and all that mattered now was the fact that no one had been killed or seriously injured in the explosion.

"I'll call you in a couple of days."

BAYLOR REINED IN TEXAS high on the ridge above the ranch house and studied a set of animal tracks he'd been following since noon. Bessy, his oldest and most seasoned cow dog, had taken off from the house last night chasing something and hadn't returned.

"Bess!" he yelled for the umpteenth time, pausing to listen for any sounds that might lead him to her.

He spurred Texas forward, following the tracks

until they veered off the game trail and disappeared into the soft bear grass that covered the exposed hillside.

A knot fisted in Baylor's gut as he stared at the trail ahead of him. Clearly pressed into the soft soil was a shoe print. He rode up on it and climbed down out of the saddle.

Squatting beside it, he traced it with his finger. It was a man's boot. Right foot, he guessed. There were traces of the left boot track but it was partially off the trail and into the grass, pointed in the same direction as Bess's paw prints where they left the path.

Someone had been up here last night watching the ranch below. Old Bess had caught their scent.

The hair on the back of his neck bristled as he stood and mounted up. He rode along the path a little farther, but didn't find any human tracks. Whoever had been up here last night was savvy enough to cover their trail.

Caution laced through his veins as he turned Texas around for the descent off the mountain. He'd have to keep an eye on his dog Buck or risk having him disappear, too.

Halfway back to the ranch he spotted Mariah's car coming up the driveway. She'd decided to take him up on his offer? Moving Texas into a slow canter, he covered the distance quickly and slowed his horse as she climbed out of her car and leaned against the door.

The afternoon sun touched her hair and turned it

to gold in the light. She pulled off her sunglasses and looked at him, a smile on her lips. "Does your offer still hold?"

"Whoa." He reined Texas in and dismounted. A mixture of excitement and need surged in his body. He stepped toward her, not content until he could touch her. Something he had to do right now. "Depends."

"On what?" she asked, her smile dampening.

"On the terms." He tied Texas to the hitching post and strode to Mariah, pulling her into his arms. His desire ramped up and he was a goner.

"You're a man who likes negotiations?"

"No, just the foreplay around them." He pulled off his hat and put it on the roof of the car, then lowered his mouth to hers, kissing her slow and easy until he felt her respond. He deepened the kiss, letting loose a fraction of the desire thumping in his body.

Her arms locked around his neck and he pinned her to the car with his hips, tasting, touching, loving her with a primal need only she could satisfy in him.

He felt her heartbeat thud against his chest, and pulled back. Her cheeks were flushed, her lips full and soft, ready to be kissed again and again. "I missed you," he whispered.

A seductive smile bowed her mouth, but he could feel a moment's hesitation in her body as she stiffened.

"I'm taking a month off for now, but I'm considering resigning from the department. My heart's just not in it anymore...and I want to be with you."

"Are you sure? I mean…" He didn't want to wait another second, but he'd respect her wishes.

"Yeah," she said. "I want to be with you, but my experience is, well, it's… I don't have much."

Baylor felt the air bottle up in his lungs.

"I focused on college, then the police academy, then the department. I just never found the one I wanted to be with."

He brushed the hair away from her face, feeling her shiver beneath his touch as she closed her eyes.

"Sweet hell." He kissed her again, this time holding back from an all-out assault. He wanted to take her, wanted to teach her, wanted to love her.

He pulled back, out of breath and caught between a rock and a hard place. He wanted her now, but he would wait until she was ready to give him what she'd saved for one man. Willingly and without hesitation.

"Come on, let's take a ride. I've got a couple of stray steers up on the east ridge I'd like to herd down. And I'd like to take a look at the mine entrance where we came out."

Mariah nodded, glad for the distraction and the time to let her out-of-control emotions step back in line. Baylor was a true gentleman, but that wasn't the side of him she'd wanted to unleash.

"Not sure if I can ride with this." She held up her casted arm. "But if we were to get stuck in there again in the dark, this could show us the way home."

Baylor grabbed his hat off the roof of the car and

shoved it on his head. "You can rein one-handed, can't you?"

"Yeah." She gazed at him, relishing the view, from the slant of his stubble-darkened jaw to the contemplative gleam in his eyes, and her heart beat faster, sending tentacles of anticipation rocketing through her.

"We interviewed Rachel Endicott today." Baylor took her hand and steered her toward the corral, where Jericho stood eyeing them.

"Get anywhere?"

"She knew about Amy and James's affair." His grip tightened on her fingers.

"I'm sorry. I realize that's an unpleasant subject for you."

He pulled her to a stop and turned into her. The air was filled with a tension so intense she could feel it vibrate between them.

"It's in the past, Mariah, and I can't live there anymore. Amy is dead, there'll be no question-and-answer session. There are things I'll never know, but as much as it riles me, I've accepted it."

"I'm glad." She searched his face, relieved when he smiled down at her. "Things can only get better from here. No more dips in the emotional dunk tank."

A laugh rumbled in his throat and she felt the dark cloud lift.

"I once volunteered to sit in the dunk tank at the country fair. Good thing there weren't many Girl

Scouts with good aim in my line just waiting to see my cowboy hat bob up on top of the water. But I did get wet."

"Was it for a good cause?"

"Yeah. The local fire department needed a new truck."

Baylor pulled the lead rope from over the corral gate and undid the latch. He snagged Jericho's halter, clipped on the shank and led him out to the hitching post where a saddle sat on the end of the rail.

Mariah felt useless as she watched him brush the big bay gelding. "Can I get his bridle?"

"Yeah. In the tack room on the rack with his name carved on the front."

Mariah took off for the tack shed next to the corral. She pulled open the door of the ten-by-ten shed and smelled the scent of leather and fly wipe.

A long shaft of sunlight pierced the darkness inside and allowed her to spot the bridle hanging on a rack at the back of the structure.

She stepped inside.

A quake of caution shook her as a flash of movement on the floor next to her right foot caught and held her attention.

Recognition and terror registered at the same time a scream gurgled up her throat.

Baylor heard it. Sharp and high-pitched, coming from the tack shed.

"Mariah!" He dropped the horse brush and raced

for the shed, his mind searching for a cause to her distress. Had she injured her broken arm again, pulling the bridle down off the rack? Dammit, he shouldn't have let her attempt to get it.

He swung the door wide and stared inside.

Mariah stood in the middle of the room, frozen in place. On the floor in front of her a rattlesnake lay coiled, ready to strike. A second snake slithered near her right foot, unconcerned, as he inched past her.

Caution locked on Baylor's nerves. If he approached and tried to move her, chances were good she'd get bitten.

Beads of sweat pearled on his forehead. "Hang on, sweetheart."

He spotted the saddle pad lying over Jericho's saddle, and the straight-edged shovel propped next to the shed door.

In slow motion he took several steps back and grabbed the thick pad. Keeping his eye on the snake, he moved forward, locking his hand around the handle of the shovel.

The snake remained coiled and ready to strike at any second.

Taking a deep breath, Baylor tried to relax as he stepped into the tack room. The movement drew the snake's attention. Baylor stepped in front of Mariah and wheeled the pad like a shield.

The snake struck out at him, hitting the pad and sinking its fangs into the foam.

Mariah bolted and jumped on top of a saddle rack, out of the line of fire.

Before the snake could release and strike again, Baylor smacked it with the blade of the shovel and flung it out of the open door.

Turning his attention to the second snake, he again used the thick saddle pad as a shield, and wrangled the snake with the shovel, scooping it up and shoving it out the door.

Baylor snagged Mariah, and raised her into his arms. With the shovel as a weapon, he turned and left the shed, depositing her a safe distance away, watching to make sure the rattlers continued their frenzied exit into the tall grass behind the shed.

"One snake, I'd believe, but two?" He scanned the hillside looking for movement. "I was in there this morning. It was clear. Someone put them in there, knowing I'd be back to stow my saddle."

He reached out and pulled Mariah into his arms.

"I hate snakes," she said.

"Come on now, they were just little guys."

She whimpered. "Little, big, any size in between. I hate them all."

Mariah finally succeeded in losing the willies the snake encounter had given her, but not until Baylor had reentered the tack room for Jericho's bridle and they were mounted up high off the ground.

"How would someone corral those rattlers?" she asked as she rode along next to Baylor.

"A snake hook. You'd wrangle them from their den and put them in a sack. I didn't want to tell you, but if you'd been bitten by both of them, you'd be dead."

She shuddered. "Well, then, I'm glad you showed up when you did. Any idea who might have put them there?"

"Bess, my old cow dog, went off last night chasing something on the slope. I found a boot print up there this afternoon."

Taking a cursory scan of the hillside, she tried to relax but couldn't. "You told me once that strange things had been happening on the ranch. What kind of things?"

"Loose lug nuts on my pickup three times, including the morning I took you up to the hospital. A couple of one-ton hay bales dislodged in the barn last winter and just missed me. Someone has been in my house a couple of times, including the night I brought you in from the storm. And the night we found Endicott in the barn and the gun in the tea pitcher. The front door wasn't locked."

"Did you ever file a report?"

"And say what? I think someone's trying to kill me?"

"Yeah. And what about the shots someone took at us up by the pond? We believed it was Ray Buckner, but I never got to question him. Do you think he saw whoever did it?"

"It's possible. Maybe that's why he was tossed into the bull pen. To shut him up."

Uneasiness sparked through Baylor's veins like lightning. Were they dealing with a local? Someone who moved about undetected because he blended in?

Maneuvering down onto the road, they covered the distance to the trailhead into the pond.

Baylor worked his horse through the trees, using the forest as cover. They couldn't risk becoming targets again. He didn't relax until he pulled Texas up short ten yards away from the mine shaft opening, and dismounted, helping Mariah down and tying up her horse.

Raising his finger to his lips, he warned her to be quiet. Listening, he focused on the sounds emanating from the woods around them. Woodpeckers, the hum of crickets and wood beetles. A mild breeze hissing in the pines overhead.

Reaching out, he took her left hand and moved toward the opening. Buck brush as high as his thigh protected the entrance along with the massive log. Baylor paused. Something wasn't right. The entire forest seemed to be holding its breath, but for what?

He took a step forward, feeling a slight pressure against his shin. He froze midstep and stared down at the thin thread of wire holding him back.

He'd just set the trigger. "Stop," he whispered to Mariah. "Go back, the area is booby-trapped."

Mariah almost bumped into Baylor, who stood

like some kind of a statue in front of her, but she hesitated, honing in on the last word of his sentence. *Booby-trapped.*

Slowly, she pulled her hand out of his and took two careful steps back. She stared at the ground in front of him.

The sun glinted off a fine strand of wire.

"Don't move," she said, following the line to where it vanished into the brush. Raising her gaze, she felt like she'd been hit by a bus when she spotted a line of steel-tipped arrows pointed directly at Baylor. One wrong move and he'd release the volley.

"There's an entire quiver of arrows aimed at you. How much pressure can you feel in the trip wire?"

"It's tight. The trigger is set."

"Can we drive something into the ground to hold it long enough for you to get out of the way?"

"Maybe." Baylor stared down at the line stretched across the boot of his right foot. They'd be hard-pressed to find anything that would exactly match the pressure his foot exerted against the trip wire.

"Can you reach the arrows?"

"Yeah. I think so."

"Whoever put this here had to load the device. You have to unload it."

He didn't dare turn to look at her, but he could feel her eyes on him as she considered the task.

"If I don't do it correctly—"

"You will." *You have to.* He let the rest of the

thought die on the breeze. If all else failed, he planned to hit the dirt in front of him, and hope like hell that the arrows passed overhead and missed them both.

He heard her moving through the buck brush and closed his eyes. "Nice and slow, Mariah. One arrow at a time."

"Okay. What sort of a maniac does this kind of stuff?"

"He's desperate. Desperate to protect this mine site."

"Okay, I'm here. It's a round disc with five arrows in it. Each in its own cylinder."

"How high off the ground is it? Is it angled? And how far away is it?"

"It's a foot off the ground, tipped at a five, maybe ten-degree angle, and fifteen feet away from you."

Dread thumped in his body. The booby trap would deliver five kill shots to his body's core, if it triggered.

"Don't touch the arrows. It's too dangerous. It could release if you touch it. Go around it to the other side, see where the wire goes in."

The brush rustled as she moved around the weapon. "I found it. It's tied to a trigger of some sort."

Baylor's heartbeat hammered in his ears. Beads of sweat rolled down his back between his shoulder blades, and he forced air into his lungs, feeling it calm his nerves.

"I want you to put tension on the trigger, the same amount as the wire is holding. That should give me enough time to step back and hit the ground. Then let it go."

"Are you sure?"

"We don't have a choice." He turned his head slowly and stared at her, then nodded the go-ahead.

He saw her exaggerated swallow and prepared to get the hell out of the way of the barrage.

Mariah knelt down next to the weapon, a silent prayer on her lips. Reaching out with her left hand, she placed it on the backside of the trigger, duplicating the pressure holding the trigger forward.

"Okay. I'm holding it."

"On three, I'm going to step back."

Fear ripped through her as she held the trigger. It had to work, or Baylor was as good as dead. The razor-sharp arrows would drill holes in him.

Glancing up, she watched the top of his head as he stepped back. The trigger gave a fraction, but the arrows didn't launch.

"Clear!"

She let go of the trigger and ducked to the left.

The volley shot out of the weapon and sliced through the air, driving into several trees on the opposite side of their trajectory.

Mariah raced for Baylor, who lay sprawled under a low scruffy pine. She dropped to her knees and planted a kiss on his mouth.

"Come here." He pulled her down next to him. "Look up there, what do you see?"

She followed his line of sight, her stare locking on the huge pine where the booby trap had been mounted. "It's a camera."

"Yeah. It seems the SOB likes to watch his kills."

Anger raced in her veins. She stood up and moved toward the camera, careful to stay out of its sight. Reaching down, she picked up a bulky limb, crept up and smashed it to pieces. "One for the good guys."

Baylor stood up, ready to get back to the ranch. There could be more cameras pointed at them right now, and they couldn't risk coming across any more surprise weapons.

"Let's go." He took Mariah's hand and they headed for the horses.

THEY RODE IN SILENCE up the driveway, and stopped next to the corral.

"Hey, look at that," Mariah said as she climbed off her horse.

Baylor trained his attention on the mountain behind the ranch house, where a ring of ravens circled, a couple at a time swooping to the ground.

A knot formed in the pit of his stomach. "That's where I saw the boot print. We better check it out. It could be Bess."

He waited for Mariah to remount Jericho and spurred Texas forward, pushing him into a canter, only slowing once they started up the mountain on the game trail. He hoped like hell it wasn't his dog.

Mariah pulled alongside him, ducking under a pine bough.

The clamor of birdcalls signaled that they'd reached the area, and Baylor slowed his horse. Mariah dropped in behind him and stopped.

"Whoa." He dismounted and dropped the reins, ground-tying the horse. "Stay put."

Mariah nodded and stroked Jericho's neck.

Baylor moved to the top of the rise and peered over. There, less than a hundred yards from the spot where he'd turned around that afternoon, he saw Bess.

He bolted for her, scattering the scavengers before they could devour her.

"Dammit, Bess." Baylor dropped to his knees beside his dog, fighting a rush of emotion. Reaching out, he touched her side, and started when she raised her head and looked at him.

Excitement surged in his veins. "You're going to make it, Bessy. Come on." Carefully he scooped her up into his arms and took off for his horse.

Chapter Ten

The veterinarian, Mike Sanders, came into the waiting room. "She made it, but she's going to need recovery time. This was in her left shoulder." He reached into the pocket of his lab coat and pulled out a small baggie, holding it up to the light. "Bullet. A couple of centimeters lower and it would have nicked her heart."

Baylor took the baggie and handed it to Mariah. "She's a good dog, saved my butt more than a couple of times."

"I'd like to keep her for a few days. Make sure she heals properly. We'll give you a call as soon as she's ready to be released."

"Thanks, Doc." Baylor reached out and shook the veterinarian's hand before he and Mariah left the clinic.

"It looks like a .38 slug. The striations are visible." Mariah opened her hand with the bagged bullet. "Whoever Bess was chasing on that mountain was armed."

Caution rattled through Baylor as he digested the information. It wasn't uncommon for anyone to be packing a pistol in this countryside. Hell, he did most of the time. You never knew when you might need it to protect yourself from a predator, or put a wounded animal out of its misery, but shooting a man's cow dog bordered on certifiable.

Baylor focused his attention on the dark gray thunderclouds building on the horizon. "Looks like we're in for a storm. We better get back to the ranch and batten down the hatches."

Mariah nodded and pulled open the pickup's door. She climbed in and buckled up.

Baylor slid in behind the wheel and fired up the truck. "We never got that banana split the other day." He glanced over at her and watched her smile. Damn, he loved that.

His feelings for her raged through him like wildfire and he had to look away. Did she feel the same? Baylor sucked in a breath, put the rig in Drive and pulled out of the parking lot, headed for Ruby's Diner.

MARIAH TRIED TO SEE the road through the swipe of the wiper blades and wondered how Baylor was managing. The violent thunderstorm had broken wide-open just as they'd left the main highway and started up the Salmon River road. Night was falling, accelerated by the black clouds overhead. Tension bunched her muscles and frayed her nerves, but she trusted Baylor.

She watched him flip his headlights onto high beam and trained her eyes on the gravel road ahead.

Deluges were never welcome in the backcountry. They loosened rocks from the hillsides, sent mudslides down through the steep narrow draws, and made the rivers and streams swell exponentially without warning.

"We'll be lucky if the lights are on when we get home." Baylor slowed down and steered around a jagged rock the size of a cooler, sitting in the middle of the road.

Nervousness held her body prisoner as they rounded a curve and drove through a swollen creek that had maxed out its culvert and pushed onto the roadway in its rush to reach the river below.

"Relax, sweetheart." Baylor glanced over at her and her tension melted. "We're almost home."

She liked the sound of that. The Bellwether did feel like home to her for some reason. But she could call any place home as long as he was beside her.

Lightning hissed across the night sky, illuminating everything in its arc. Thunder roared, shaking the truck with its deafening vibration.

A chill skittered over her body as she saw the pines lining the road bend in the gale force winds that drove the rain in sheets.

The milepost marking thirteen miles loomed in

the glow of the headlights. A quarter of a mile to go before the turn into the Bellwether Ranch.

Baylor stayed focused on the road in front of him, feeling the steering wheel in his hands telegraphing the road conditions meeting the pickup's tires. They were skating on mud that was as slick or slicker than ice and a lot less forgiving. Once it sucked you sideways it'd be hell pulling it back.

The bolt of lightning flashed white-hot in front of the truck, blinding him in the process. Sparks hissed and popped up where the strike burned into the tree, frying sap and moisture.

In an instant the ponderosa split and launched forward.

Instinctively, Baylor pulled the steering wheel to the right, dumping the pickup into the ditch and just missing the tree as it crashed down right next to them.

A limb slammed into the front windshield. It shattered.

Mariah screamed.

Baylor yanked the wheel hard to the left, popping them out of the ditch and back onto the road, but the truck couldn't get any traction.

He let off the gas and rode the brake.

The pickup rocked back and forth as the brakes caught and held, but not soon enough.

In one last lurch forward, the nose of the truck dropped over the embankment, pointed down toward the river. The only thing that prevented it from taking the plunge was the pine acting as a balance.

Mariah sat so still she could hear her heart pounding in her eardrums.

The wipers made a pass over the shattered windshield, clearing enough liquid that she could see the raging river below in the glare of the headlights.

It took everything she had not to jump from the pickup.

"You okay?" Baylor asked, his voice just above a whisper.

"Yeah."

A low moan of stressed steel was followed by a jerk as the pickup inched forward, and stopped. The pine tree was still holding them, but not for long.

"We've got to get out. Unbuckle your seat belt."

Reaching down, Mariah fiddled with her belt, mentally willing her hand to stop shaking. It popped open, and she reached for the door latch.

"We have to go out the back window. I'm not sure we're even resting on the bank. The soil is loose. You could step out and it could give way."

Baylor was right. She heard his seat belt open.

In her peripheral vision she saw him reach for the automatic window control panel, and heard the rear window glide down. Instantly the violence of the raging storm filled the pickup, lashing her hair and whipping it against her face.

He turned the key and the engine went silent. "I

want you to go first." He glanced over at her. "Take your time. Move slow. Stay on the back bumper, and for God's sake, jump if it starts to go."

Mariah felt a wave of denial push through her. How could she leave him? How could she live with watching him go over the embankment and vanish in the black water below?

She couldn't move. Terror locked her in place. Was this how Baylor felt the night he'd tried to save Amy? Helpless?

"Go, Mariah! Go now!"

She pulled her legs up and turned in the seat.

The truck creaked, rocking gently in time with her movements.

Rising up, she came to a crouching position and touched Baylor's cheek with her hand.

He turned into her palm and kissed her. "Go. Please. We haven't got much time."

The burn of tears flamed behind her eyelids and her throat constricted. In that instant she knew she loved him, and that she could lose him in seconds.

Easing up, she put her left leg through the open rear window. Lowering it until she felt the bed of the truck beneath her foot.

In a smooth motion, she jockeyed the rest of her body out behind it, careful to keep her weight moving forward until she reached the back of the pickup bed and climbed out onto the bumper. "I made it. Now you go," she yelled over the howl of the wind.

Silently she prayed that Baylor would make it out alive. That he'd beat the physics of the situation. She needed him. And then he was next to her, helping her down off the bumper. She felt her heart lift in her chest as she threw her arms around him.

"Come on, I've got to anchor the truck."

"How?" She followed him to the opposite side of the road and watched him attempt to shove a large bolder with his foot. "This one will work."

Reaching down, he rolled the rock up out of the ditch and together they pushed it until they reached the rear wheel of the pickup.

Baylor slid it in front of the passenger's-side rear wheel and knocked it in tight. "That should hold it until morning."

He took her hand and she sagged against him, content when he put his arm around her and turned her toward the ranch.

Leaning into the wind, they made the turn into the driveway and pushed for home.

Biting rain pelted her cheeks and racked her body with chills, but half an hour later, Baylor was pushing open the door to the house and locking the storm out.

He flipped the light switch in the entry. Nothing. "Stay here."

While he went to get a light, Mariah peeled off her soaked clothes a layer at a time, until she stood shivering in her bra and panties, watching him move around the house lighting candles and the fireplace in the bedroom.

"That was my job," he said from behind a flickering candle when he finally approached her.

Warmth spread through her, quieting the chills. He'd removed his jacket and shirt and stood barechested in front of her. Her body responded and desire ignited in her blood, drawing her to him like a magnet to steel.

Baylor set the candle down on the console table next to the front door and pulled her against him, feeling the burn of her skin against his.

It was familiar, but new. This time she was conscious and her skin was anything but cold. With his hand he grasped her chin and tipped her face up. Staring down into her eyes, he looked for the hesitation he'd seen there before, but it was gone. His heart hammered in his chest as he kissed her, his hunger growing with each passing second.

He broke the kiss and scooped her up into his arms. She settled against him as he carried her through the doorway of the bedroom and pushed the door shut with his bare foot.

The fire had warmed the room and set it aglow with firelight that softened and touched her skin. His desire raged out of control as he laid her down on the bed, watching her face as he shed his wet jeans and boxers, then climbed on the bed next to her.

Her cheeks flamed, a signal that she'd recognized the level of his need. He moved over the top of her, grasping one of her bra straps and pulling it down before kissing her shoulder, tasting her skin.

The other strap was next and he felt her pull back for an instant. He gentled his seduction and she relaxed, closing her eyes as he undid the front clasp of her bra and pulled it aside, exposing her breasts in the firelight.

"You're so beautiful," he whispered, his mouth going dry.

A half choke, half moan came from between her parted lips and she opened her eyes, stared up at him.

"I want you."

What was left of his doubt melted along with his heart, and he lowered his mouth to hers. "I want you back." He kissed her, with slow, deliberate tenderness, working to control the desire that threatened to burn him up from the inside out. Making love to her was his only desire. Teaching her, pleasuring her.

Outside, the roar of the thunder matched the escalating crescendo in her body as Baylor ran his hand down her side and hooked his fingers inside the waistband of her panties, pulling them down over her hips, before he hooked his foot in them and dragged them down her legs and off.

He pulled the nipple of her left breast into his mouth, teasing it with his tongue until she thought she'd writhe out of her skin if he didn't appease her growing frustration.

Reaching down, she brushed her fingers through his hair as he lined up kisses down her midriff, across her belly button, and ending where no man had ever touched her before.

Ecstasy ignited a fire inside her and the rhythm of his tongue added emotional fuel to the heat. A gush of pleasure rocked her, releasing the tension that held every muscle in her body prisoner, and then he was there, pressing her against the soft sheets, his eyes dark and filled with longing as he stared down at her. She opened for him, causing him to moan as he brushed against her.

She was ready. Ready to love him, with her heart and her body.

MARIAH ROLLED ONTO her side and thrust her good arm over the spot where Baylor should be, but wasn't. Slowly she opened her eyes and caught sight of him standing next to the window, staring out into the darkness.

The firelight emanating from the hearth burned low and danced across his naked skin. She drank him in, from the muscular build of his shoulders tapering down to his narrow hips, and well-shaped thighs. Every cell in her body wanted him at the same time.

"Come back to bed," she said softly.

He pulled the blinds and turned toward her, a sultry smile on his lips. Lips that had kissed her senseless for hours.

The gentle patter of rain on the roof was the only sound in the room. The rage of the storm had passed, leaving peace in its wake, much the way their love-making had begun and ended.

Baylor pulled back the covers and slid in next to Mariah, gathering her in his arms. He wasn't sure what had woken him, maybe the low-pitched howl he'd heard from somewhere on the ranch, or maybe just the fact that he shared his bed with her. No matter the reason, he was satisfied, but needy. Content, but hungry for more.

He closed his eyes, breathing in the sweet scent of her hair. He'd loved Amy, but not like this, not with the intensity that churned inside of him and drove his emotions further and faster than he'd ever thought possible.

Desire coursed through him as she turned in his arms and spread kisses against his throat. He hardened instantly and rolled her beneath him.

Dawn could wait.

MARIAH HELD THE telephone receiver to her ear for the fourth time in two hours and finally heard a dial tone stream across the line. The smell of bacon and coffee excited her taste buds as she dialed her father to check in.

"Sheriff's department."

"Chief Ted Ellis. Please."

"One moment."

"Ellis here."

The sound of her father's gruff voice made her

smile and she longed to tell him her news. Well, most of it anyway. "Daddy."

"'Bout time you gave your old man a call. Things have been hopping around here."

Her interest was piqued. "The case?"

"Rachel Endicott came in yesterday afternoon with her lawyer in tow. I interviewed her, we charged her and arrested her this morning."

"Arrested her, for killing her husband?" She glanced at Baylor, who stood frozen in the kitchen. He set down the plate he was holding and moved toward her.

"No. We're holding her on a felony vehicular manslaughter charge for now, if it doesn't get reduced."

Confusion laced through her brain. "Vehicular manslaughter? Who?"

"Amy McCullough."

Mariah's breath caught in her throat and nothing would come out for a moment as she tried to link the facts. "How?"

"Get your tail to the station, you can watch the interview…bring Baylor along. He needs to hear this, too."

The line went dead in her hand and she replaced the receiver, feeling like she'd been hit by a bus.

"What the hell?" He put his hands on her shoulders.

Mariah looked up into his face. "Rachel Endicott

has been charged with vehicular manslaughter in Amy's death."

A look of surprise widened his eyes for a moment. "How?"

"I don't know, but my dad wants us both to listen to the interview ASAP."

"I'll get dressed." Baylor headed for the bedroom and she followed along behind him, trying to put it all together. Dammit, she'd never even seen this coming.

BAYLOR COULD SWEAR there wasn't a liter of air in the viewing room as Chief Ellis put the VHS tape into the recorder. The ride into town had been hell on his nerves and worse on his memories of that night.

Near as he could tell, he'd been the one behind the wheel. He'd been the husband who couldn't swim. He'd let her slip away and hadn't been able to go after her, but nowhere in the scenario did Rachel Endicott fit, not physically, and not mentally.

Ellis pushed the start button and snagged the remote. "Came as a hell of a surprise to me." He pulled up a chair next to Mariah and leaned back.

"State your name and date of birth for the record."

"Rachel Jean Endicott. February twenty-second, nineteen seventy-two."

"I'm going to assume you're here with your lawyer to tell us about the disappearance and murder of your husband, James Charles Endicott?"

She glanced at her lawyer then back at the camera. "No."

Rachel Endicott cleared her throat, and took a drink of water from a glass sitting on the table. "No. I want to talk about the night Amy McCullough died."

Dread seeped from deep inside of Baylor's body, his muscles pulled tight, and he strained to hear the next words coming out of Rachel's mouth.

"I tampered with her car in the parking lot of the Steak House that night." Rachel's voice quivered with emotion. "I didn't know her car would go off into the river... I didn't know I'd kill her. She was messing with my husband. I only wanted to scare the hell out of her. I wanted her to stop tearing my family apart." A choked sob shook her body and a hand appeared at the edge of the screen holding a tissue.

Rachel took it, dabbed at her eyes and took another drink from her glass.

"You're aware that you've admitted to a vehicular manslaughter charge?"

"Yes, sir. I am."

"Can you tell me specifically what you did to Amy McCullough's car and how you believe that caused her death?"

"I come from a family of auto mechanics. It's amazing what you can do with an eleven-dollar ball joint and tie rod separator fork. I broke the press fit on the bolt, pulled the carter key and screwed the nut back on with a couple of threads. It vibrated loose…and that's when the McCulloughs went into the river."

Baylor felt like he'd been kicked in the gut. He stood up. He'd felt the damn thing snap when he'd yanked on the steering wheel to avoid hitting the deer. Anger and relief intertwined in his body.

"I was driving, Chief Ellis. I was driving that night and I felt it pop. I can testify to the fact."

"I didn't find that in the statement you gave." The chief hit Pause on the video recorder remote and came to his feet, followed by Mariah, who stepped between the two men.

"He told me the truth, and I believe him. It doesn't make any difference who was behind the wheel that night. Amy is still dead, and now we know Rachel Endicott caused the accident. Don't we?" Mariah stared at her father and saw sympathy soften his features.

He didn't say another word, just hit the play button. The machine clunked and continued.

"So you knew about the affair between your husband, James, and Amy McCullough?"

"Yes."

"How did you find out about that affair, Mrs. Endicott?"

Rachel dropped her head forward and rubbed her

eyes, then straightened and pulled in an audible breath. "I found some pictures in my husband's briefcase one morning."

"And what was the subject matter in the pictures?"

"Him and her, screwing around." Rachel cleared her throat and took another drink from her water glass. "The bastard couldn't deny it. I asked him to stop seeing her, but he said he wanted a divorce." She made a loud sniffing noise and mopped at her nose.

"What did you do with the pictures, Mrs. Endicott?"

"He took them away from me, and put them back in his briefcase. I didn't see them again until after he disappeared. They were in the bottom drawer of his dresser, but you've got the same ones."

"What do you mean?"

"I saw them when Detective Ellis put them out in front of me at the interview."

"Do you know who took them?"

"No."

Her lawyer, Deiter Pruett, laid his briefcase on the table and opened it, pulling out an envelope. "You'll find the photos in here, Chief. We'll turn them over if you promise to lessen the charge."

"Now, Deiter, you know I can't promise anything without the prosecutor's consent."

"Give them to him. I feel bad enough about what happened to Amy. Just give him the damn pictures. Now!" Rachel's face contorted and she rubbed at her eyes.

Deiter promptly handed the envelope over to the chief. "Will you be charging my client?"

"Yes. But I have one more question. Do you know where your husband was going on April fifth, Mrs. Endicott?"

Rachel looked down at the floor, "No, sir. I don't have a clue."

Mariah felt her blood pressure shoot up. "She's lying. Look at her body language. That's the only question she answered with her head down. She couldn't look at you, Dad, because she's being deceptive."

Ted Ellis paused the tape. "I'm with you. Maybe she had him killed and framed Baylor so she could get off the hook."

Mariah considered her father's suspicion, but couldn't quite buy into it. They were still missing something, something huge.

A knock sounded at the door of the viewing room and the door was pushed open. A uniformed officer poked his head inside.

"Chief, I thought you might like to know that Judge Moorehouse reduced the charge to a misdemeanor and cut Rachel Endicott loose half an hour ago on bond. She's picking her things up right now in booking."

"Dammit! Get an unmarked car on her pronto. Don't let her out of your sight."

"You've got it." The door closed with a bang

behind the officer and Mariah felt the tension in the room explode.

"I want in on this. We want in on this." She nodded toward Baylor.

"In case you've forgotten, honey, you're on leave. Go home." He turned to face Baylor. "Take her home, son. I've got a notion that's where her heart has been anyway."

Chief Ellis left the room with a slam of the door.

"He's right, Mariah. This could get ugly. Rachel Endicott is a desperate woman. Let the police handle it."

Baylor was right, her father was right, but she couldn't shake that tiny niggling in the back of her mind.

They'd missed something, or someone.

Chapter Eleven

"Play it back again." Mariah sat in the dispatcher's office, clinging to her notion that there was someone else involved in Endicott's murder.

"911, what is your emergency?"

"Fire. Bellwether Ranch." The first garbled 911 call ended.

"911, what is your emergency?"

"The barn's on fire at the Bellwether Ranch. Hurry." The line went dead.

Baylor cocked his head, his eyes narrowing. "Can you play the first call again?" he asked.

The technician respooled the tape and hit the play button for the eighth time.

"Fire. Bellwether Ranch."

"Do you recognize the caller?"

"I can't be sure but it sounds like my neighbor, Harley Neville, after he has had a few drinks at the Long Branch. The second caller is my ranch hand, Travis."

"Is there any way to clean up the first call?" Mariah asked.

"I can clear out some of the background noise, amplify the voice, but I can't do anything about the quality." The technician sat back in his chair.

Mariah glanced at Baylor. "We can go and talk to him. See if he reported the fire, too."

"It's worth a try, but so what if Harley called it in. He drives past the ranch every day in order to reach his place. There's nothing suspicious about it. He saw the flames and phoned it in."

"Thanks." She nodded to the technician and they left the dispatch center. Baylor had a point, Neville did drive by the ranch every day.

"Maybe it was a murder for hire," she suggested.

He pushed open the door for her and they stepped out into the afternoon sunshine. "Could have been, but there's too much drama. Why not just have him shot and buried?"

"And then there are the pictures. The mates to the ones we received. Which means our set most likely came from whoever was blackmailing Endicott."

Baylor stopped her beside the car and touched her cheek. "Stop, Mariah. Stop second-guessing everything. Your dad will figure it out."

"I hope so." But she couldn't silence the nagging dread that leaked from her bones and tainted her thoughts. Two people were dead, Endicott and Ray Buckner, three if she counted Amy whose involvement wasn't clear, and maybe never would be. Then there were the ongoing attempts on her and Baylor's lives.

"Let's swing by the vet's, see if we can pick up Bess."

"Sure." Mariah tossed the keys to him and climbed in the passenger's-side door feeling dissatisfied.

BAYLOR GLANCED OVER his right shoulder at Bess, who lay on a towel in the backseat of Mariah's car. It felt good to be taking her home.

"I've got something for you." He cast a sideways glance at Mariah, who stared out the open car window, watching the scenery flit past as the breeze moved her hair.

She looked over at him. "A surprise? I like a good surprise, as long as it's not rattlesnakes, gas explosions or a slick road."

He refocused ahead, feeling his heart beat faster and his palms begin to sweat.

They rounded the curve before the ranch entrance and Baylor braked, then came to a stop next to Harley Neville's pickup.

"What the…" He put the car in Park and climbed out.

Harley met him halfway. "Damn lucky you didn't take the plunge. I thought I'd help you out by getting your rig back on the road."

"Thanks." Baylor stared at his pickup and the

heavy chain Harley had secured to the rear axle. The truck was now parked on the edge of the road, feet away from where they'd left it teetering last night.

"I tried to start it to move it up to your place, but the battery's dead."

"I had to leave the lights on." He could have shut them off, but they'd been the only constant light source, and pitch-black would have terrified Mariah even more.

"I can tow it up your driveway."

Baylor reached out and shook Harley's hand. "No, thanks. I'll bring the tractor down later and tow it to the house so I can put a charge on the battery."

"Sounds good." Harley moved away to unhook the chain from the axle.

"I owe you one." Baylor snagged the keys out of the ignition, shoved them into his pants pocket and climbed back inside the car. He put it in Drive and eased past on the right side.

In the backseat, Bess's ears perked up and she sat up, her nose sniffing the breeze blowing through the open window next to her.

A low growl rumbled in her throat and raised the hair on the back of Baylor's neck.

Had she caught the scent of a predator? There were plenty to contend with. Cougars, bears and wolves.

He pulled into the head of the driveway and

braked hard as a mother bear and her cub trekked across the road in front of them.

"Look at that," Mariah said from beside him. "I'd like to capture them on canvas."

"There's nothing stopping you now."

She smiled at him. "I lost everything in the explosion. I'm going to have to make a trip to the art supply store after I find a place to live."

"Yeah." He squeezed the steering wheel a little harder and curbed a grin.

Why was he so tense? Mariah wondered while she watched him maneuver the car up the road and ease into the parking spot in front of the garage.

"Stay put." He climbed out of the car, opened the rear door and let Bess out before coming around to the passenger's side to open her door. She couldn't take another second of it.

"Okay, what's going on?"

He took her hand and helped her out of the car. "Just come with me."

Excitement latched on to her insides as she followed him around the side of the house and into the backyard where a large table was positioned and covered with a sheet. Next to it was a standing easel, which was also covered.

"I know how much this passion means to you, Mariah. And I want you to explore it. I picked up a few things after your house went up." Baylor pulled the sheet off the table, uncovering a selection of artist's supplies that would make Vincent van Gogh jealous. It was everything she'd lost, and more.

Mariah's throat tightened and she stepped into Baylor's arms, breathing him in, feeling happiness overtake her.

"Thank you."

"There's more."

She pulled back and stared up into his eyes. The twinkle of anticipation she saw there made her smile. "This is great. I don't need anything else."

"I do." He sobered and she felt her heart jump in her chest as he led her over to the standing easel and pulled the sheet off, exposing a large blank canvas.

She looked at it, her gaze locking on the bottom right-hand corner. Her throat tightened and she mentally traced each letter. There, written in oil paint was the artist's signature, Mariah McCullough.

"Stay, Mariah. Let me love you." Baylor's words soaked into her stunned mind and took hold. He wanted her to marry him, he wanted her to be his wife?

"Yes," she whispered. "Yes."

He pulled her against him and she reveled in the feel of him. Breathed in his outdoorsy scent. Listened to his heart beat in his chest as he held her like he'd never let her go. She was home, she realized when he scooped her up in his arms and headed for the front of the house.

"A ceremonious carry over the threshold?" She relaxed in his arms, and breathed him in.

The clatter of thundering horse hooves drew her attention to the driveway.

Riderless, Jericho galloped up the drive and bucked to a stop in a cloud of dust and gravel.

Baylor sobered and set Mariah down.

He bolted to the winded horse, who stood heaving, his nostrils flaring.

Baylor's gut knotted with tension as he circled the horse Travis had ridden off on this morning.

His gaze locked on the darkened leather of the saddle. Reaching out, he brushed his finger against it and pulled it back.

Blood.

He heard Mariah's gasp, and turned toward her, but she was already running down the driveway.

He took off after her, spotting what she ran toward.

Travis lay in the middle of the driveway, not moving.

Dread leaked from Baylor's bones as he sprinted and stopped beside Mariah, who sat on the ground next to Travis, trying to get him to talk to her.

He'd been severely injured. His face was almost unrecognizable. Several huge gashes covered his head. He wasn't responding to her questions, and he was bleeding profusely.

"I'm going to call an ambulance."

Mariah nodded, and went back to work trying to revive him.

Baylor raced for the phone and help.

THE ROTOR BLADES WHINED and stirred up dust as the medical helicopter lifted off the driveway and took off for the hospital with Travis on board.

Baylor held Mariah next to him, watching and praying the kid made it. He tensed with caution. Without Travis to tell them what had happened to him, they had no way of knowing if it was an accident, or if someone had caused his injuries.

He released Mariah and headed for Jericho. The horse flinched as he approached, going wide-eyed and nervous.

"Easy," he coaxed, moving in slow, before stroking the horse's neck.

"Is he okay?" Mariah asked, standing next to him as he checked the horse over with his hands.

"Yeah. But he's still shaking. He's a seasoned horse. Whatever happened to Travis up there couldn't have been good."

Mariah worked her way around Jericho, looking for anything that might hint at what happened, but besides the blood on the right side of the saddle, there was nothing.

"Do you suppose he came in contact with a booby trap?"

She saw Baylor swallow, his eyes narrowing as he

worked out the scenario in his head. "Could be. Dammit, I should have ridden out and seen if there were more."

She brushed his arm. "So you could be a victim, too?"

Pain flashed in his eyes. "Who would do this? He's just a kid, like Ray Buckner was just a kid. Did your CSI ever come up with anything in his case?"

"It was ruled an accident, but I think he was pushed in just like I was."

He had to agree, as he unsaddled Jericho and brushed him down before turning him out into the pasture.

The Bellwether Ranch had become a dangerous place to be, a fact that stirred anger in his blood and made him more determined to find the SOB responsible, before anyone else got hurt.

Chapter Twelve

Baylor pulled up the reins of Texas's bridle, grabbed the saddle horn and mounted up. "We've got an hour before dark. Plenty of time to search out a couple of strays I saw up the ravine this afternoon."

Mariah was next to him on Jericho, looking as cowgirlish as he'd ever seen her. He smiled as she glanced down at the engagement ring on her left hand for the umpteenth time, then back up at him with a broad smile on her lips.

His heart jumped into his throat. She was so beautiful, and so much his. Reaching out, he stroked his hand down her cheek, seriously considering a horse race to the house and over the finish line to the bedroom. Desire, hot and heavy, sluiced in his veins. He was going to need a lifetime to prove how much he loved her.

"Whoa, cowboy," she said, a laugh in her throat. "Save it for after dark. We've got cows to herd."

He let his hand drop to his side and smiled. "Slave driver."

Turning Texas, he spurred him forward, and Mariah fell in next to him.

The evening air was cool and crisp, loaded with the scent of new grass, pine and syringa. He'd asked her to marry him and she'd said yes. The solitaire on her finger had belonged to his grandmother. Everything was perfect, save the unanswered questions in the Endicott case, and his ranch hand lying in a coma in the hospital. But he didn't doubt that Ted Ellis could handle things.

Glancing over at her, he wondered if she could really hang it up so easily for her artwork and him. He was certain there was a part of her that would always be a cop, even after she turned in her letter of resignation tomorrow.

They reached the end of the driveway and Baylor glanced at his pickup, still parked where Harley had dragged it. He planned to hook on to it with his tractor in the morning and tow it home.

The roar of a car engine racing up behind them jolted his nerves. Grabbing Jericho's reins close to his bit, he hurried them off the road and into the ditch, just as a red BMW zipped by without slowing down.

He recognized that car; he'd seen it once before.

"Damn, she almost hit us." Baylor reined in Texas and stopped. "That was Rachel Endicott. Where the hell is she going?"

"I don't know, but she's in a hurry. What's up there?" Mariah asked.

"Harley Neville's place."

Caution took hold of Mariah's senses and she nudged Jericho up out of the ditch and onto the road. "Come on, we've got to follow her."

She spurred the big bay horse into a lope, bent on tracking Rachel Endicott. Where was she going, and what was she doing racing toward Harley Neville?

BAYLOR TIED TEXAS to a low branch and helped Mariah secure Jericho.

There was no moon in the night sky, and the darkness was thick. Only the light coming from Harley's front porch fixture acted as a beacon, guiding them to within a hundred feet of the house.

Caution put Baylor's senses on high alert. Instinctively he reached for Mariah's hand, feeling the urge to protect her. From what, he didn't know, but something was out of place. Harley Neville and Rachel Endicott just didn't go together. What was their relationship?

Baylor listened for sounds coming from the house, but heard nothing. No voices, no dog barking, nothing.

"Wait." He pulled Mariah to a stop. "Something's not right. Harley's dog Charlie should be coming unglued right now. You can't get within a hundred feet of this place without him going off."

"Maybe he's inside."

"Maybe, but let's stick to the shadows until we figure out what's going on."

"Okay."

Together they worked their way up the driveway, passing Rachel's BMW and Harley's pickup in the process, before taking cover behind a lilac bush flanking the left side of the sidewalk.

The front door of the house gaped open halfway. "That's weird," Baylor said, increasing the pressure on her hand.

Mariah agreed, wishing she'd taken the time to strap her pistol on, but it was back at the Bellwether. "They could be having a nice conversation about the weather."

"Let's just walk up to the door, Mariah. Knock, holler and go inside. I mean, what's Harley going to do? Tell us to get out, mind our own business?"

Mariah pulled in a breath. He was right. If Rachel Endicott wanted to visit Harley Neville, that was her business, but considering she was a suspect in her husband's death, a possible murder for hire, the situation suddenly seemed anything but benign.

"I'm going in," Baylor said, stepping out onto the walkway. She fell in next to him and followed him up the front steps to the open door.

"Harley! It's Baylor, you in there?"

He pushed the door open, exposing the inside of the house.

Mariah pulled in a quick breath.

The place was trashed.

She moved to step through the entrance, but Baylor held her back.

"I don't like this. Whoever took this place apart might still be inside."

She agreed, but they had to call for help and try to find Rachel and Harley. "I'll stay put if you want, but one of us needs to get help." She eyed the telephone on the wall next to the kitchen door. "You search for them and I'll call 911."

She could tell by the way he narrowed his eyes that he didn't like the situation, but that he knew she was right.

"Harley," Baylor shouted as they moved over the threshold and into the abandoned house.

Caution buzzed through her. She stepped around a smashed lamp that had been swept from a table. The drawers of a desk hung open, paperwork lay scattered on the floor around it.

"Baylor." Mariah trained her eyes on a photo lying in the pile of papers. "Look at this."

She picked the picture up by the corner, a wave of fear crashing inside of her.

"Damn." He was next to her, and she fought the urge to cling to him.

"He's been watching us." Baylor stared at the photo taken through the bedroom window the first night they'd spent together.

Dropping his gaze to the floor, he squatted, shuffling through the paper until he found another picture. This time he wasn't surprised as he stood up and handed it to Mariah.

He heard her audible intake of breath. "He took the pictures of James and Amy. He was blackmailing Endicott. But why? What did he have to gain?"

Tension gripped Baylor. "I don't think he was blackmailing Endicott. He was blackmailing Amy."

Mariah struggled to get her thought processes around the bizarre turn of events. "But why? What hold did he have over her?"

"There's one way to find out. Harley!" Baylor bellowed, setting her nerves on edge. Moving quickly, she pulled the receiver from its cradle on the wall.

No dial tone.

Fear etched a path along her spine and she realized they were totally alone. They had to run. To get back to the ranch.

Foreboding locked its tentacles around her heart and began to squeeze. Was Harley dangerous? Was Rachel a threat? She certainly was capable of malice. She's used it to tamper with Amy's car the night she died.

"Harley!" Baylor's voice cut into her thoughts as she watched him move down the hallway and through the house, searching the bedrooms one by one, before he strode back to her side.

"It's empty. There's no one here. But they

couldn't have gone far. We were only half an hour behind Rachel, and we didn't see them on the road."

"Damn, would you look at that?" Baylor scrounged in the pile of papers, pulling out the one that caught his eye.

"What is it?"

"A topographical map of the Bellwether." He focused on a series of tiny circles along the property line separating Harley's property from his. He knew the area well. It was just outside of the meadow, but he rarely rode herd that far east. The terrain was too rugged and too dangerous for grazing.

"That's right." The sound of Harley's voice, along with the hammer being pulled back on a pistol, sent a jolt of anger through Baylor.

He wheeled, positioning Mariah behind him.

"It's the Bellwether, and every one of those circles represents millions of bucks." Harley plastered a phony smile on his fat lips. "I would have shared."

"Shared?" Baylor pulled in a breath; the puzzle was beginning to come together.

"You really don't get it, do you?" Harley stepped closer and jerked the map out of Baylor's hand before moving back out of arm's reach.

"I'm bloody rich. Once you and the lady cop are dead, I'll have unlimited access to the gold that's on your property. I've already dipped into it, got the assay reports to prove how rich it is."

The smile dropped from his face and his features

hardened. "I could have been enjoying it sooner if Amy had just gone along."

Baylor's hearing perked up, momentarily scooting back his plan of attack. "What's she got to do with any of this, Harley? She's dead."

"She'd agreed to help, with a little persuasion."

"The pictures of her and Endicott?"

"Yeah. Funny how that worked. I followed her to talk to her about what I'd found, but there she was, sucking face with a public servant." He snorted. "I couldn't resist. I grabbed my camera and snapped a couple of shots, then followed them to the motel."

Harley shook his head. "She made it too easy, and when she refused to screw you out of that half of the ranch in a divorce settlement, I gave her the pictures along with a copy of the assay report."

A knot balled in Baylor's gut. "You're a bastard, Neville."

"I didn't know she'd hand it over to Endicott." A flash of regret shone in his eyes. "And then she was gone, but you made it out alive. It wasn't long after that James Endicott was up in my face. He promised he'd put you away, and demanded a cut of the profits for silence about the find, but you were cleared of wrongdoing and he had nothing. Still he wanted in and threatened to tell you everything. I couldn't let him. It was mine. All mine. I had to kill him."

Harley took a step back. "I've tried to kill you

both. God knows I tried plenty of times, but you always managed to make it through."

Baylor didn't like the way Harley leered at Mariah, and he reached for her behind his back. Instead of making contact with her body, he felt a metal object as she laid it against his palm and folded his fingers around it.

The letter opener from the desk he'd pinned her to in his attempt to shield her from Harley's gun.

"What about Ray Buckner? You killed him, too?"

"He saw me the day I took those potshots at you up in the meadow. I couldn't let him talk and ruin everything."

Harley took another step back and pointed the gun a couple of times to the front door. "Don't make this hard, McCullough. Out, both of you."

Baylor closed the distance to Harley in two steps and lunged for his arm to deflect any bullets.

"Run!" he yelled to Mariah, catching her in his peripheral vision on the right as she darted into the kitchen and toward the back door and freedom.

The letter opener slipped out of his hand as he tried to subdue Harley, but he was stronger than an ox.

Silently he prayed she didn't play cop, didn't endanger her life. But his hope didn't manifest; instead she came barreling out of the kitchen wielding a knife.

Harley's eyes went wide, and Baylor sensed him pondering his next move.

The hammer clicked, the blast from the gun exploding near his ear. The wayward shot pounded into the ceiling above his head, raining down particles of plaster.

"Dammit, Mariah, get out!"

She froze and turned tail back into the kitchen. Not for a better weapon, he hoped, but to save her life.

Mariah stumbled out the back door of the house, trying to see in the darkness. Her eyes adjusted even as she put together the remnants of a plan. The letter opener and the knife were no match for a bullet. She'd have to find something else to use to take Harley out.

She stepped off the porch and tripped over something.

Plunging headlong, she hit the ground hard. The air pushed out of her lungs as she dragged herself up onto her knees.

A shaft of light from the open kitchen door knifed into the darkness, pointing its beam directly at the object she'd stumbled over.

A wave of nausea slammed into her and she covered her mouth.

Rachel Endicott lay flat on her back, in a pool of blood, her face to the sky, a bullet hole in her forehead.

Panic set Mariah's nerves on fire and shoved her to her feet, more determined than ever to stop Harley.

The light glinted off Rachel's right hand.

Keys. The keys to her car. She'd run it straight through Harley's damn house.

She grabbed the keys, jerking them out of Rachel's lifeless fingers, and bolted around the side of the house, bent on doing whatever it took to save the man she loved.

Chapter Thirteen

Pop.

The sound of a single gunshot froze Mariah in place.

Who'd been hit? Was it Baylor? Or Harley?

Fear rioted inside her, betraying her hope that the situation would end in their favor.

She couldn't live without him. She didn't want to try.

Pulling in a ragged breath, she focused on the car, its outline visible in the darkness, and ran toward it.

From the corner of her eye she saw movement. In a desperate attempt to get away, she jumped sideways, but he was too quick, and in one lunge, Harley Neville slammed into her, forcing her to the ground.

She rose up and found the barrel of the gun jammed against her forehead.

"Nice try, but I'll blow you brains out if you move."

She swallowed the terror that consumed her and tried to focus on staying alive.

"Stand up," Harley ordered, coming to his feet.

Slowly she did as she was told, and he jerked Rachel's keys out of her hand.

"Move." He shoved her toward the car, then opened the passenger's-side door. "Get in."

Mariah climbed into the car, but it was too late to act by the time she saw the pistol butt coming at her and heard the crack.

A jolt of pain slammed into her skull behind her right ear and darkness consumed her.

THE SOUND OF RUSHING water somewhere in the distance rained into Baylor's dazed mind. His head throbbed and he tried to open his eyes, breathing in the smell of gunpowder.

He probably had it on his clothes. The last thing he remembered was fighting over the gun with Harley. Then the gun went off…

Wincing, he raised his hand to his head, making contact with the matted hair, still moist with blood. He'd been shot, only grazed and still alive. Mariah! Where was Mariah?

His heart rate climbed and he became fully conscious at the instant he felt a jolt and heard the grind of metal on metal.

Where was he? Dragging his eyes open, he stared into the darkness, reached out and touched the steering wheel.

Damn, he was in his disabled pickup.

A barely audible moan sounded from the passenger seat and, reaching out, he felt Mariah next to him.

Another jolt, this time the truck inched forward.

Realization dawned on him and pulled all of his scattered thoughts into solid understanding, but it was too late.

Baylor crushed the brake pedal, pushing it as hard as he could.

The roar of Harley's truck as he accelerated was deafening.

The pickup slid forward, wheels locked as Harley pushed them closer to the edge.

Panic hissed through him. He popped the transmission into Park, but it wasn't enough to stop the process.

The pickup's nose dropped over the edge of the embankment in the same spot it had the night of the storm.

In slow motion Baylor watched the tree that had held them bend forward from the force and vanish under the truck.

Horror knotted his stomach and he reached over and grabbed Mariah's hand. It was that night all over again, the night Amy died. Baylor closed his eyes and waited for impact in the cold dark water below.

It came seconds later. Hard and fast.

Blindly he pulled himself up using the steering wheel and kicked forward, hitting the already shattered windshield. "Mariah! Mariah, we've got to get out."

Icy water spilled into the cab of the truck, sucking his strength.

"Mariah!" He searched the darkness for her. Feeling around on the passenger's side, he found nothing.

"God, not again." He couldn't lose her.

A flash of neon-pink in the dark water outside of the sinking pickup caught his attention. He pushed off the dash of the truck, lunging for the beacon in the water.

Mariah's cast.

He locked his hand around her wrist and kicked for the surface. He broke through and pulled in a breath, angling Mariah's head above water so she could breathe.

The current had them. He didn't try to fight it, just let the river carry them downstream to a calm section of water.

The intensity lessened and Baylor began to stroke the water with his arm, just like he'd taught himself. Stroke and kick, stroke and kick. Focused on the dark shadows of the bank.

He felt the bottom come up under his feet, and carried Mariah in to shore, collapsing on the riverbank. Exhausted, he held her close, unsure what Harley had done to her.

"Mariah." He shook her. "Mariah!" Panic bulldozed his insides. He couldn't lose her.

"Baylor." Her voice in his ear finally calmed him.

"I'm right here. What did he do to you?"

"Pistol-whipped."

"Bastard. We've got to go for help."

She nodded, then abruptly stopped, putting her hand

to the side of her head. "He thinks we drowned. He's trying to make it look like an accident. He killed Rachel Endicott. She was lying out back. He shot her at point-blank range. She must have known Harley was the last person her husband talked to. Too bad she kept that information to herself. She might still be alive."

"Dammit." Caution took hold of him, and he stared into the darkness, listening for any sign that Harley waited for them, but the rush of the river upstream covered any sound coming from the road a hundred feet above.

"We've got to keep moving. Can you walk?"

"I think so. How'd you get me here if you can't swim?"

"I can, now. After Amy drowned, I went to the pond every day. Wore a path to it and drank most of it, but by the end of last summer I knew how to swim."

Mariah's heart jumped in her chest as she considered the courage it took to do that, and she was thankful he had.

Baylor helped her to her feet, and together they started the laborious climb up the steep bank, over rocks and brush until they lay on their bellies next to the side of the road.

She tried to quiet her breathing, which seemed loud in her ears. She didn't want to draw attention. She didn't doubt that Harley would do whatever it took to kill them this time. He had millions of reasons.

The shuffle of boots on gravel made her go silent.

From out of the darkness a flashlight was turned on, its beam catching them both in the face.

"Son-of-a-bitch," Harley yelled, just as Baylor pulled her back.

Harley aimed his pistol and began firing.

Bullets pinged against rocks, and pounded into the dirt next to them.

"Keep him busy," Baylor said in her ear.

Mariah rolled to the right and Baylor moved left. Terror pushed her forward, but her training took over.

She counted Harley's shots. Five already, six-round cylinder in the .38, one more shot.

"Now," she yelled.

The last bullet fired out of the gun and Baylor tore into Neville, hitting him from the left side.

Somewhere in the darkness a rifle shot rang out.

Harley flinched, but both men went down.

Horror inflamed Mariah's body and she bolted up onto the road.

Where had the shot come from? Was Baylor hit?

Staggering the last three feet, she collapsed in the dirt next to him.

Harley Neville lay dead in the road, the flashlight still in his hand, and a shot through his chest.

The flash of emergency lights came around the bend in the road.

Baylor came to his feet and Mariah fell into his arms, staring at him in the headlights of the police car. He pulled her close.

Officer Kirby, the local deputy, strode toward them, a rifle with a nightscope resting on his shoulder. "Are you both okay?"

"Yeah. How did you find us?" she asked.

"Your dad put an unmarked car on Rachel Endicott after she made bail. He followed her to the river turn and called for backup. McCullough's ranch hand, Travis Priestly, regained consciousness this afternoon, and told us Neville attacked him with a hammer. The lab found Neville's prints all over the photos Rachel turned over at the station. He was in the system on an old trespassing case."

"Rachel Endicott is dead. She's back at Harley Neville's place in the backyard. He killed her." Mariah leaned into Baylor, enjoying his warmth. Their clothes were still wet, but she could feel his heat against her skin.

"We better get you both into the ambulance and warmed up." Officer Kirby raised his hand and waved to the emergency vehicle that had stopped just back from the scene.

Mariah couldn't agree more as she stared up at Baylor, knowing he planned to keep her warm for a long time. "I love you," she whispered, feeling her insides rush with heat.

"I love you, too," he said as he lowered his mouth to hers.

Epilogue

One year later

"Hurry, we don't want to be late," Baylor said from the bedroom.

Mariah glanced out of the bathroom door and watched him as he attempted to knot his tie. He looked good in a suit, but she liked him better in boots and a hat. Just boots and a cowboy hat.

"Sweetheart, will you help me with this?"

She dropped the pregnancy test wand sporting a giant plus sign into the trash can and left the bathroom.

"Sure." She easily wrapped the long end around and pulled it through the knot, before she cinched it up to his collar. "You look great."

A hungry look passed across his face, and a sly smile tugged on his lips. "So do you."

She turned in her dress, watching the skirt flail out around her. Tonight, after the gallery opening party and the reserve sales, she would tell him they were going to have a baby. Just the thought made her smile until she thought she'd bust.

"What's up?" he asked, his blue eyes narrowing with contemplation.

"I love you."

He stepped toward her and her heart squeezed. She had everything she'd ever wanted. A husband she loved more than life itself, a gallery filled to the brim with her paintings, and a child growing inside of her.

His child.

"We'll just have to be late." He pulled off his Stetson, and she reached for his tie.

* * * * *

Harlequin is 60 years old, and Harlequin Blaze is celebrating!
After all, a lot can happen in 60 years, or 60 minutes...or 60 seconds!
Find out what's going down in Blaze's heart-stopping new miniseries,
FROM 0 TO 60!
Getting from "Hello" to "How was it?" can happen fast....

Here's a sneak peek of the first book,
A LONG, HARD RIDE
by Alison Kent.
Available March 2009.

"Is that for me?" Trey asked.

Cardin Worth cocked her head to the side and considered how much better the day already seemed. "Good morning to you, too."

When she didn't hold out the second cup of coffee for him to take, he came closer. She sipped from her heavy white mug, hiding her grin and her giddy rush of nerves behind it.

But when he stopped in front of her, she made the mistake of lowering her gaze from his face to the exposed strip of his chest. It was either give him his cup of coffee or bury her nose against him and breathe in. She remembered so clearly how he smelled. How he tasted.

She gave him his coffee.

After taking a quick gulp, he smiled and said, "Good morning, Cardin. I hope the floor wasn't too hard for you."

The hardness of the floor hadn't been the problem. She shook her head. "Are you kidding? I slept like a baby, swaddled in my sleeping bag."

"In my sleeping bag, you mean."

If he wanted to get technical, yeah. "Thanks for the loaner. It made sleeping on the floor almost bearable." As had the warmth of his spooned body, she thought, then quickly changed the subject. "I saw you have a loaf of bread and some eggs. Would you like me to cook breakfast?"

He lowered his coffee mug slowly, his gaze as warm as the sun on her shoulders, as the ceramic heating her hands. "I didn't bring you out here to wait on me."

"You didn't bring me out here at all. I volunteered to come."

"To help me get ready for the race. Not to serve me."

"It's just breakfast, Trey. And coffee." Even if last night it had been more. Even if the way he was looking at her made her want to climb back into that sleeping bag. "I work much better when my stomach's not growling. I thought it might be the same for you."

"It is, but I'll cook. You made the coffee."

"That's because I can't work at all without caffeine."

"If I'd known that, I would've put on a pot as soon I got up."

"What time *did* you get up?" Judging by the sun's position, she swore it couldn't be any later than seven now. And, yeah, they'd agreed to start working at six.

"Maybe four?" he guessed, giving her a lazy smile.

"But it was almost two…" She let the sentence dangle, finishing the thought privately. She was quite sure he knew exactly what time they'd finally fallen asleep after he'd made love to her.

The question facing her now was where did this relationship—if you could even call it *that*—go from here?

* * * * *

Cardin and Trey are about to find out that great
sex is only the beginning….
Don't miss the fireworks!
Get ready for
A LONG, HARD RIDE
by Alison Kent.
Available March 2009,
wherever Blaze books are sold.

CELEBRATE
60 YEARS
OF PURE READING PLEASURE
WITH **HARLEQUIN**®!

We'll be spotlighting a different series
every month throughout 2009
to celebrate our 60th anniversary.

Look for Harlequin® Blaze™ in March!

0-60

*After all, a lot can happen in 60 years,
or 60 minutes...or 60 seconds!*

Find out what's going down in Blaze's
heart-stopping new miniseries *0-60!*
Getting from "Hello" to "How was it?"
can happen fast....

Look for the brand-new 0-60 miniseries in March 2009!

www.eHarlequin.com   HBRIDE09

HARLEQUIN® *Romance*®

This February the Harlequin® Romance series
will feature six Diamond Brides stories featuring
diamond proposals and gorgeous grooms.

Share your dream wedding proposal and you could WIN!

The most romantic entry will win a diamond
necklace and will inspire a proposal in one of
our upcoming Diamond Grooms books in 2010.

In 100 words or less, tell us the most romantic
way that you dream of being proposed to.

For more information, and to enter
the Diamond Brides Proposal contest, please visit
www.DiamondBridesProposal.com

Or mail your entry to us at:

IN THE U.S.: 3010 Walden Ave., P.O. Box 9069, Buffalo, NY 14269-9069
IN CANADA: 225 Duncan Mill Road, Don Mills, ON M3B 3K9

www.eHarlequin.com   HRCONTESTFEB09

REQUEST YOUR FREE BOOKS!

2 FREE NOVELS PLUS 2 FREE GIFTS!

HARLEQUIN®

INTRIGUE®

Breathtaking Romantic Suspense

YES! Please send me 2 FREE Harlequin Intrigue® novels and my 2 FREE gifts (gifts are worth about $10). After receiving them, if I don't wish to receive any more books, I can return the shipping statement marked "cancel." If I don't cancel, I will receive 6 brand-new novels every month and be billed just $4.24 per book in the U.S. or $4.99 per book in Canada, plus 25¢ shipping and handling per book and applicable taxes, if any*. That's a savings of close to 15% off the cover price! I understand that accepting the 2 free books and gifts places me under no obligation to buy anything. I can always return a shipment and cancel at any time. Even if I never buy another book from Harlequin, the two free books and gifts are mine to keep forever.

182 HDN EEZ7 382 HDN EEZK

Name	(PLEASE PRINT)	
Address		Apt. #
City	State/Prov.	Zip/Postal Code

Signature (if under 18, a parent or guardian must sign)

Mail to the Harlequin Reader Service:
IN U.S.A.: P.O. Box 1867, Buffalo, NY 14240-1867
IN CANADA: P.O. Box 609, Fort Erie, Ontario L2A 5X3

Not valid to current subscribers of Harlequin Intrigue books.

Want to try two free books from another line?
Call 1-800-873-8635 or visit www.morefreebooks.com.

* Terms and prices subject to change without notice. N.Y. residents add applicable sales tax. Canadian residents will be charged applicable provincial taxes and GST. Offer not valid in Quebec. This offer is limited to one order per household. All orders subject to approval. Credit or debit balances in a customer's account(s) may be offset by any other outstanding balance owed by or to the customer. Please allow 4 to 6 weeks for delivery. Offer available while quantities last.

Your Privacy: Harlequin is committed to protecting your privacy. Our Privacy Policy is available online at www.eHarlequin.com or upon request from the Reader Service. From time to time we make our lists of customers available to reputable third parties who may have a product or service of interest to you. If you would prefer we not share your name and address, please check here. ☐

HI08R

The Inside Romance newsletter has a NEW look for the new year!

Same great content, brand-new look!

The Inside Romance newsletter is a FREE quarterly newsletter highlighting our upcoming series releases and promotions!

Click on the Inside Romance link on the front page of **www.eHarlequin.com** or e-mail us at insideromance@harlequin.ca to sign up to receive your FREE newsletter today!

You can also subscribe by writing to us at: HARLEQUIN BOOKS
Attention: Customer Service Department
P.O. Box 9057, Buffalo, NY 14269-9057

Please allow 4-6 weeks for delivery of the first issue by mail.

You're invited to join our Tell Harlequin Reader Panel!

By joining our new reader panel you will:

- Receive Harlequin® books—they are FREE and yours to keep with no obligation to purchase anything!
- Participate in fun online surveys
- Exchange opinions and ideas with women just like you
- Have a say in our new book ideas and help us publish the best in women's fiction

In addition, you will have a chance to win great prizes and receive special gifts!
See Web site for details. Some conditions apply.
Space is limited.

To join, visit us at
www.TellHarlequin.com.

Coming Next Month

Available March 10, 2009

Spring is here and romance is in the air this month
as Harlequin Romance® takes you on a whirlwind journey
to meet gorgeous grooms!

#4081 BRADY: THE REBEL RANCHER Patricia Thayer
Second in the **Texas Brotherhood** duet. Injured pilot Brady falls for the
lovely Lindsey Stafford, but she has secrets that could destroy him. Now
Brady must fight again, this time for love....

#4082 ITALIAN GROOM, PRINCESS BRIDE Rebecca Winters
We visit the **Royal House of Savoy** as Princess Regina's arranged
wedding day approaches. Royal gardener Dizo has one chance to risk
all—and claim his princess bride!

#4083 FALLING FOR HER CONVENIENT HUSBAND Jessica Steele
Successful lawyer Phelix isn't the same shy teenager Nathan
conveniently wed eight years ago. He hasn't seen her since, and her
transformation hasn't escaped the English tycoon's notice....

#4084 CINDERELLA'S WEDDING WISH Jessica Hart
In Her Shoes...
Celebrity playboy Rafe is *not* Miranda's idea of Prince Charming. But
when she's hired as his assistant, Miranda is shocked to learn that Rafe
has hidden depths.

#4085 HER CATTLEMAN BOSS Barbara Hannay
When Kate inherits half a run-down cattle station, she doesn't expect to
have a sexy cattleman boss, Noah, to contend with! As they toil under
the hot sun, romance is on the horizon....

#4086 THE ARISTOCRAT AND THE SINGLE MOM Michelle Douglas
Handsome English aristocrat Simon keeps to himself. But, thrown into
the middle of single mom Kate's lively family on a trip to Australia, Simon
finds his buttoned-up manner slowly undone.